ADRIAN
&
SUZETTE

WILLOW WINTERS
WALL STREET JOURNAL & USA TODAY BESTSELLING AUTHOR

From *USA Today* best-selling author, Willow Winters, comes a sexy office romance with a brooding hero you can't help but fall head over heels for … in and out of the boardroom.

I didn't get to where I am by being nice.

I'm the boss, the CEO, the owner of whatever I want. Right now, that includes every person in this building of the company I just bought.

I stop at nothing once I've decided I'm taking something.

And then she showed up … full of spitfire just for me, the man she's decided is her worst enemy.

Like I said, I stop at nothing once I've decided I'm taking something. This pretty little thing just moved to the top of my "must acquire" list.

TELL ME
YOU
WANT ME

PROLOGUE

ADRIAN

"Can you believe how we started?" Suzette questions, her voice barely above a murmur. I've gotten used to her whispers this late at night. It's nearly midnight now. I've gotten used to far too much because of her. This room, on the top floor of the most coveted skyscraper facing Bryant Park, has been hell every morning when the partners arrive. When they leave, and most of the lights turn off, and Suzette hesitantly knocks on the large walnut door to my office ... it's been nothing but heaven.

As if I would ever turn her away. As if I could possibly deny myself, let alone her.

"Can I believe how we started?" The low timbre of my

voice carries an echo of her question, a chill flowing along my shoulders as the air conditioner switches on. My gaze slips to the dark wood flooring barely lit by a single lamp in the corner of the office. Then it falls to my silk tie atop the puddle of Sue's cashmere blouse, both items thrown carelessly on the floor. She's still naked, completely bared to me, although I've pulled up my slacks. I relax into the high-back chair, my bare skin against the leather, and watch Sue reach for the bottle of scotch. The glasses clink together when she grabs them next. Her pale rose nipples are soft now that she's sated and the sight of them persuades me to run my thumb along the pad of my pointer, desperate to toy with her and bring them back to hardened peaks for me to suck and pluck, forcing more of those delightful sounds from her cherry-red lips.

As she turns slightly from where she's lying across my desk, the dim lights of the city shine through the large paned glass windows and cast shadows along her tempting curves. She is my safety, my temple of solitude, my everything. At this moment, I'm far too aware of what she means to me.

"Yes," she speaks confidently, raising her voice as the amber liquid is poured into the first glass. "I was just thinking that I never would have imagined we'd have ..." she pauses, her chest rising and falling with a single breath before carefully placing herself in front of me. The bottle sits to the left of her, and both glasses are to the right. "This," she finishes. With Suzette seated on my desk, her bare feet planted on my chair between my spread legs, her ass balanced on the edge and her breasts directly at my eye level, I have to tilt my chin up to meet her gaze.

The little vixen smirks. She knows what she does to me. I didn't even realize I'd fallen for her until it was too late.

It was nothing more than a game at first. I don't know when it all changed and turned into "this," as she put it. I don't know when it became what it is, but now that I have it, I don't want to lose it.

Can I believe how we started? Did I know it would turn into this?

"No," I say, giving her the answer I know she wants to hear. Her simper and huff of a laugh warm the coldest depths of me, but they're quick to freeze the moment she hands me the cut crystal tumbler of whisky.

I sip it regardless, because she wants me to and because as I do she indulges herself, relaxing and confiding in me. It's all I want, for as long as I can have it.

She has no idea that everything is going to change only hours from now. I'm the only one suffering of the two of us. I can only imagine the betrayal she'll feel tomorrow when the headlines reveal the truth in black and white.

With the soft hum of a satisfied woman, Suzette leans forward, lowering her lips and positioning them right there for the taking. The glass landing with a hollow *thunk* on the maple desk is the only sound in the room besides the raging of my blood pounding in my veins. A moment passes, the heat blistering in her gorgeous gaze as if she can see through me. My stomach sinks and a sick feeling takes over in only a split second as her head tilts and an unasked question seems to linger at her lips.

I act before I let on that anything is wrong. My kiss is nothing shy of ruthless. I don't hold back a damn thing. I take exactly what I want from her because I know, in the depths of my soul, it will be our last time together. Tomorrow, she'll want nothing to do with me. Nipping her bottom lip, I take advantage of that sweet mouth of hers when her lips part with a provocative moan.

"I want you again," I confess to her in a low groan that rumbles up my chest. Both her hands have gripped my shoulders so it's no surprise when her nails dig into my skin and she calls out in surprise as I grab her ass off the edge, pushing her back flat against the desk so I can take her again as I have a dozen times or more.

I have to have her at least once more. One more time where she's mine. Where we have *this* ... before I lose it all when the sun rises.

CHAPTER 1

ADRIAN
SEVERAL WEEKS EARLIER...

My polished Oxfords smack on the sleek marble tile. The floors are the only thing that look expensive in the foyer of this building. It's old and dated just like their business practices. But that's all about to change now that I'm in charge.

Although I keep my expression neutral, maybe cold, as I make my way to the elevator and then to the top floor where the conference room is located, I smirk to myself as I hear the soft whispers and see the secretaries huddling together.

They know who I am. Everyone who's *anyone* does.

Asshole. Prick. Hell, I've even been called a villain. And I couldn't care less.

I pull at the sleeves to my suit and fix my cufflinks before opening the glass door. A dozen people instantly still as I walk into the room, one swivel chair squeaking as everyone goes silent. The conference room smells like the lemon polish the cleaners use on the large oval mahogany table.

That'll be the first thing to replace. The table needs to be glass so I can monitor their body language with every meeting. My father says I was blessed with two gifts: reading people and placing bets. As a gambling man with a head for stocks and companies, I know damn well he was right. And I've left a sea of people who hate me for it in my wake.

I didn't get to where I am by being nice.

I'm the boss, the CEO, the owner of whatever I want. And right now, that includes every person in this building. Straightening my tie, I remind myself I'll have to cull the herd sooner, rather than later. For the sake of both profits and efficiency. The numbers never lie; people always do, though.

"Good afternoon," I say, greeting them as Mr. Holt stands from his spot just to the right of the head of the table, which is empty. No one's seated there because it's reserved for me.

"Mr. Bradford, it's nice to see you again," Jonathan Holt says as he shakes my hand. He's the former owner and now a wealthy man.

A nondisclosure agreement was signed. No one knew I've been the acting CEO for the last quarter. Every email, every camera feed, every contract and meeting was passed through my team. They had a quarter to prove to me this company is worth salvaging.

Not that Holt gave a fuck. He was getting paid regardless. With a tailored gray suit and fresh shave, he's already a lighter, wealthier man than he was when I first met him six months ago to negotiate this deal.

As my eyes skim across each of the members I've invited for this meeting, half likely to stay, half likely to leave, a gorgeous woman catches my interest. She's in a skintight, bloodred dress that matches her perfectly manicured nails. I've seen her wear it before, if I'm not mistaken. Twice, and this makes the third. The third time is the charm.

I already know who she is before she dares to stare back at me with an openly hateful look.

Suzette Parks. Passionate. Dedicated. And hot as hell. I can't help the smirk that slips into place when she meets my gaze directly, daring me to call her out. I've witnessed her lose her patience, all alone in her office, on the brink of losing it. Entertaining isn't enough of a description. I wanted nothing more than to push her against the wall and fuck the frustration out of her. My cock stirs just thinking about how her nails would dig into my back. She's wound tight but not easily shaken. No matter what happens to this company, I'll be damn sure to keep stock of my little vixen.

She's the first to back down and break eye contact. At the same time, the door closes behind me thanks to Mr. Holt, and it signals the beginning of the meeting.

My smile widens and I cover it with my fist, clearing my throat and getting a grip. I knew she'd distract me, I knew she'd get under my skin but I wasn't prepared to be this ... off-balance.

I begin, still standing, and Mr. Holt follows suit. He nearly takes his seat but stands upright when I speak. "I'll make this short. Last quarter was unimpressive and changes will be drastic. That will include layoffs and budget cuts, but is not limited to other necessities. I will rely on each of you selected from your teams for this advertising management firm." I meet all eleven of them eye to eye as I speak. Noting which ones nod, and which ones tense up. I'm not surprised in the least until I get to Ms. Parks, who doesn't bother to peer up. As I speak, her attention is on the pen in her hand. It's an ink pen with a sleek silver body and it silently taps against her leatherbound book. No notes are being taken.

My voice is harder when I state, "I don't believe in failure. Even mistakes are lessons." The quote I've heard her say a dozen times in the last month rewards me with her icy blue gaze. That's better.

I hold her there, pinning her down as I let a second pass and then another. I can practically feel the temperature rise in the room as she struggles not to squirm. The fucking table should have been replaced already.

"Unless you have anything you'd like to say, Mr. Holt," I say and gesture toward the man. He shakes his head, his thin lips pressed in a straight line. "I don't have anything to add," he states and glances across the room.

I don't miss Ms. Parks's hardened expression toward him as well. Good. I'm not the only one she blames.

"Meeting adjourned." I remain where I am, standing tall and watching them disperse while what I was supposed to say comes back to me. I have every name memorized and anger rises inside of me that I didn't make it clear to them I know every detail and statistic that matters. My jaw clenches and with that, they move faster, nodding and giving short waves as they leave.

The annoyance morphs into something else as I peer back at Ms. Parks, the pen tapping harder. She hasn't budged.

"Did you want to say something?" I question her lowly. The last two men in the room pause where they are beside Mr. Holt. Jeffries and Woods. Both were seated farthest away, both paused to my left. Woods knows what he's doing but he's far too casual with clients. I'll be surprised if the threat of a severance package turns his performance around.

In her silence, I add, "You look like you have something to say."

"Adrian Bradford," she states, looking me in the eyes and giving me a tight smile, "we all know why you're here."

For the first time today, I let my emotion come through, simply raising a brow in curiosity. "Is that so?" I ask her.

"You want the company," she says matter-of-factly and

then sits back. It's a confident move on her part as if she knows my cards.

"You're very astute," I say clearly condescendingly, and I love how she raises a brow back.

"To rip apart," she adds and then pushes her chair back, standing up and letting me finally see her curves in person. The short red dress rides up just a bit too high on her left thigh, exposing more of her skin and teasing me. I'm usually able to keep my focus, but for her, I let my gaze slip.

She yanks it down.

"Leave my department alone. I won't let anyone ruin it," she warns. Warns me. Like this is a tit for tat. Like she has any authority at all in this game we're playing.

"If I want to ruin something ..." I pause to adjust my stance slightly as I take another long look at this woman.

"You can try all you'd like, Adrian." The faint smile on her face when my expression hardens upon hearing her use my first name only adds to the insult.

"Suzette Parks, correct?"

Suzette. I taste her name on my tongue. I love everything about it, from the way it rolls off my lips to the manner in which it lingers there, tempting and taunting me.

She offers a nod and that's all, swallowing down her spite and leaving the room.

"Is she typically so ... combative?" I ask Mr. Holt as the glass door slams shut so hard that I wouldn't have been surprised if it had shattered. I haven't been on the receiving end of her wrath, but damn if it doesn't make me harder than steel for her.

Jonathan clears his throat, obviously uncomfortable as he shifts his weight where he stands, gripping the back of the chair. "I apologize, sir," he tells me, but that's not the answer to the question I asked.

"Not a worry at all," I comment, not bothering to look back at him as he rambles on. Instead I watch her go, loving that she can't get away from me. Loving that I'll be seeing more of her any damn time I please.

CHAPTER 2

SUZETTE

How fucking dare he.

How dare this man who doesn't know a single thing about me get to me the way he did? The way his piercing gaze seemed to see through me made my entire body heat. He pinned me where I stood. I felt the intensity of his hunger ignite through every nerve ending in my body, rendering me paralyzed.

I couldn't even speak, let alone look at him. It was embarrassing. Every little thing I did in that room was horribly embarrassing. I'll apologize, only because it's the professional thing to do, but I'm not backing down. My team is worth saving, worth keeping. *If he dares to fuck with me ...* I swallow thickly, knowing there's not much I can do to stop him, but he's going to hear every reason why he needs to back down before he ruins what I've spent a decade building.

I've heard rumors about him. All he does is rip apart things that aren't profitable, selling them off or merging what's worth salvaging with other companies. Adrian Bradford is a death sentence. He's my worst enemy come to life and I despise Holt for leaving me in this man's hands.

Steadying my breath, I raise my hand and form a fist at his door. One breath in, and I can't even knock. My knuckles graze the wood and I can't bring myself to do it. "Fucking hell," I mutter beneath my breath.

How has he gotten under my skin the way he has? I'm a strong woman. I pride myself on it. And yet here I am, cowering in front of a closed door.

It makes me hate him all the more.

It's not just the way he looks at me. Shaking off the anxiousness, the pent-up anger, and the desperate need to get out the rage boiling inside of me, I try yet again.

I'll blame the hell I went through last night for being so shaken.

If I wasn't so shocked, if I wasn't so sleep deprived, if I wasn't so passionate about everything that has to do with this job, storming into his office would be easy.

I know every nook and cranny of this business. When I got here, I knew nothing and quickly discovered the upper-level executives knew even less. Holt was a trust fund baby in over his head. I climbed a steep learning curve and brought my team with me.

How dare he come in here and think that he can take everything away from me? Everything that I've worked for. Everything that *we've* earned.

With an audible exhale, I nod. That's right; that's what I need to be focused on.

With another deep breath, I straighten my spine.

The image of him standing at the head of the conference table is burned into my memory. The hint of a five-o'clock shadow showing already. His dark gray, perfectly tailored suit and sharp jaw. He's like the devil—charming and wicked; threatening yet thrilling. There's a power beneath him that's undeniable. A thought creeps into my mind. Even if he was stripped bare of every expensive fabric that graced his lean but muscular frame, even then, I imagine that man would look expensive as hell. It's not wealth, it's something else. Something entirely different than what I'm used to.

All of these men can walk around in whatever designer suit they'd like but they'd still look cheap. They wouldn't know their dicks from the pens they use to sign away their inheritances. And yet here's a man, the first one I've seen in a long damn time since my divorce has been settled, who makes all of those bastards who have hit on me, who have expected things from me simply because of their bank accounts, look like the arrogant pricks they are.

Every man I've ever laid eyes on in all of New York City pales in comparison to Adrian Bradford. And I was safely surrounded by others, in the light of day, for a total of less than ten minutes.

Here I stand, outside his door, daring to get closer to him and all alone, after hours ... this door will remain wide open so long as I'm here. That's for damn sure. There's not a soul on this level and truth be told, I'm not even sure he's in this room. It's Holt's former office and the top floor was reserved for him and meetings only. So ... even if this door was open, we'd still be alone.

With my blood heating and my nerves running high, no matter how much I'd like them not to, I imagine what he'll do. I imagine Adrian saying the kind of things that have been said to me in the past by men who have held power over me, like my husband used to, and it has a completely different effect on me today than it ever has before. The very idea of it turns workplace harassment from a lawsuit waiting to happen, into late-night thoughts in bed I share with my vibrator.

Knock, knock, knock.

My hand trembles at my side, but I hold my ground.

Raising my voice, I call out, "Adrian, I'd like—" The door opens far too quickly. I'm left with my mouth hanging open, my words spoken far too loudly and the rest of whatever I was going to say jumbled at the back of my throat.

My heart races as I realize just how close to this man I

am. It's no longer a thought, it's reality. He's a man who intimidates me. Not only because of his power, of him merely being in this building and what that means. But also because of what he does to me simply by existing. It's sinful, it's wrong. I fucking hate it.

"Ms. Parks."

Fuck.

My name sounds positively sinful in the rumble of his baritone voice. His steely gaze never leaves mine as I stand there, once again paralyzed. Taking one step back, barely giving me enough room to come in, he motions with his right hand, his left hand holding the doorframe. I break the hold he has me under, shifting my attention to the wall of windows behind his desk.

They're paned windows running from floor to ceiling, and the city is vibrant behind them. I know from experience it's loud as hell far down from this high-rise. But right now, this sight could be a painting, a beautiful masterpiece of a deep blue sky turning a dusky gray with silver buildings that creep into the clouds, the yellow squares of illuminated office windows slowly bringing light to the incoming night.

I've never stepped foot in this office before. I've never been invited here by Holt, I only knew it was his office. From here on out he'll be known as the asshole who took a hefty paycheck instead of giving this company what it truly needed. Essentially, he got a get-out-of-jail-free card and we got ...

Adrian Bradford.

The room is sparsely furnished. A hardwood maple desk carved with intricate detail catches my eye first. From the smell of lemon in the air, it's been freshly polished. A dark auburn leather wingback chair sits at its head, with two high-back lounge chairs across from it.

Other than that, the vast room is empty, with blank walls that have been freshly painted as if it were brand new. In other words, on the market for the new buyer.

Anger simmers inside of me.

It's only when the door shuts behind me that I remember exactly what I'm doing here. Although the city will never cease to amaze me. I shudder at the click behind me, turning quickly to find Adrian between myself and the door. Tapping the face of his watch, Adrian tells me, "It's nearly six, Suzette."

"Suzette?" is all I can manage. There's tension between us, thick and hot.

His full lips slip into a smirk. "That's what I said." He's calm and so damn sure of himself. Everything I normally am.

"Oh, I'm Suzette now?" Even to my own ears the indignation sounds feigned. My voice quavers as I add, "Only a moment ago I was Ms. Parks."

With a single step forward, Adrian adjusts the expensive silk tie around his neck and his expansive, barren office ignites in an instant.

For a moment, a very quick moment, his icy blue gaze

drops to my lips but then they reach my eyes again before I can object to wherever his thoughts have gone. "I said it's nearly six," he murmurs. "Well, after five."

My fingers busy themselves with the hems of my sleeves. I haven't felt so nervous in ages, not since I first stepped foot in this city. All of the anxiousness that comes with starting over, starting something new that pushes you out of your comfort zone is not unfamiliar to me, although it's been a long damn time since I last felt this way. Not since my divorce was finalized.

"Is that a way to tell me to hurry up, Mr. Bradford?"

"No. Not at all. After six I have other business to discuss with you."

"After six?"

"Once work is over." He swallows and my treacherous mind focuses on the cords of his neck. The curves of it, the strength there and that masculine scent, fresh and clean with a hint of sandalwood.

"I beg your pardon, but I'm here on business."

"Yes ... other business than what we discussed this afternoon." My pulse races as he locks his gaze with mine. I can't help but to feel like the prey, already caught by a much too powerful hunter. One who wants to play with his dinner before devouring it whole.

"Other business?" Again my voice falters. I make the next statement firm. "What could I possibly want to discuss with you? Other than the threat of you simply stepping into this building." I add with indignation, "My building."

With the little courage I can muster, I lift up my chin. Feeling what I felt hours ago in that boardroom creep back into the forefront of my mind, I try to shove it down. He's no longer a sex god reducing me to a puddle of want. He's the man who threatens my very career. And for what? For statistics on the balance sheet? For the likelihood of an easy payout rather than doing the hard work?

Just as the thought hits me, Adrian checks his watch again. "It's six now, Ms. Parks."

His domineering stature abates as if he's slightly more relaxed. He reaches up to loosen his tie. The act does horrible things to my conviction.

"You're in need," he states beneath his breath. I can barely focus on his lips as his deft fingers work to undo the top button of his shirt. In one step, he's far too close and the smell of his cologne turns heavenly.

"Excuse me?" I whisper, not as confidently as I'd intended. It's darker than it was, as if the night fell around us, granting much-needed privacy.

Leaning down so his lips grace the shell of my ear, he whispers, "All you have to say is that you left something outside of this office." Shivers run down my shoulder, then lower. My nipples are already hard and I curse the fact that I haven't been touched in months for how much I want this man to do horrible things to me right now.

With my lips parted I can barely comprehend what he said. As he takes a single step back, giving me more room to think, he removes his tie completely. The silk whispers in the air as it slides against his collar. It's the only sound I can hear other than the beating of my heart. He doesn't turn around fully and he doesn't take his eyes from mine. He locks the door with one hand and tosses the tie on the floor.

"You very much have the wrong impression of me," he says and I breathe out although I don't know how. My chest rises and falls with every heavy breath I take.

"I was praying you would walk through that door," he tells me. Adrian takes a step forward with his right hand undoing the buttons of his white dress shirt one by one, starting at the top. My gaze slips down his torso, following the line of buttons to the bulge in his pants.

My God. The temperature in the room erupts.

"I was hoping you'd come see me to work out our ... differences. I was prepared to spend all fucking day listening to you rant, taking every insult with stride. I was ready to let you get it all out." For every step forward he takes, I take one step back until my ass hits the edge of the desk.

"I would be very surprised if I had the wrong impression, Ms. Parks. But I'd like to get one thing clear." With both of my hands gripping the edge of the desk, I peer up at him, bracing myself. He reaches out and brushes against my jaw with his thumb.

His touch is as commanding as his tone, his stare, every detail about him. I'm left paralyzed. Caught in a trance.

"After six o'clock, all of that shit ends and what's between us is between us." I stare into his eyes, barely breathing as he continues. "I'll say it again; all you have to do is say you've left something outside of this office." His eyes search mine and I believe him. If I were to say it, he'd back away. He'd let me leave. And then what? Would this tension be gone? Would he pretend it didn't exist?

The reality of what's happening and the consequences of the decision I'm about to make are far too real in these few seconds.

With his eyes on my lips, his thumb moves there, parting them slowly so that just the tip of his thumb presses down, enticing me to suck it. He's far too close, far too intoxicating, far too tempting.

"Have you left something outside?" he questions. That deep voice rolls through me again. I know what's appropriate in this situation. I should jerk my head back from his touch and tell him that I did leave something outside. Mention the HR complaint I'm filing against him. That's what you're supposed to do when an asshole like Adrian backs you up against his desk.

It's what I should do. I know it. And yet ... I know damn well that I want him. I want this.

The aching need between my thighs reassures me that I fucking *need* this.

Instead of answering, I move my mouth just enough to bite down on his thumb, my teeth sinking into the tip of it. The deep groan at the back of his throat is stifled and with that little movement, I force this rather dominating man to shift in front of me. "I'll need you to answer me, Ms. Parks. Because if you haven't left anything outside, I'm going to fuck you against this desk like I wanted to the second I laid eyes on you."

It's a heady feeling to bring a man like him to the point of desperation. The desire ignites in his eyes and I push him just a little further, flicking my tongue against his thumb.

His eyes close and he speaks without opening them. "Have you left something outside?"

It seems simple, in a way. He was right when he said I was in need. And letting this man do whatever he wants to me would soothe an ache I've had for days. A pent-up need that's been dying to be sated. It would be everything I've needed since I gave my ex the finger and fell down the black hole of an endless to-do list.

Of course it would. Look at him, in his expensive suit with his thumb still tracing a path on my lip and his eyes shut. He's hot. He's more than hot. He's everything I could possibly want in a man. Physically, at least. It doesn't matter that he's an arrogant asshole. I can still hate him as much as I did when I first stormed in here, but right now … I'm worked up and hot for him.

When his eyes finally open and he stares back at me with an intensity that burns inside of me just the same, I barely speak, "I didn't leave anything outside."

Before the last word is spoken, his lips are on mine, devouring them. Both hands cup my face, pulling me in and my hands splay against his broad chest. He's all man beneath the suit. Strong muscles bulge and tense.

The layers of fabric between us are in the way and I do my part to help strip them off. Adrian isn't hesitant about a damn thing. His hands roam, his lips mold against mine and with every small movement I make, he meets it tenfold. I don't think a man like him is capable of being timid about anything. He puts his tongue in my mouth, glides it against mine, and seems to taste me more deeply than any man ever has before. Wanting more and forcing small sounds from me as his hands roam and the zipper is pulled down my back. The chill of the air greets my bare skin and I have to break the kiss, breathing in the cool air as I arch my neck and throw my head back. Adrian doesn't stop, doesn't pause for anything. His nimble fingers work my dress, sending goosebumps down my skin where his fingertips leave traces of his heated touch.

As I stare up at the ceiling, he leaves a trail of openmouthed kisses down my neck. Hot and greedy, it's enough to pull me back to him.

To rid myself of any thoughts other than those drenched in lust.

Scorching desire prickles over my skin and I find myself kissing him back, maybe a little desperately. Shamefully so. I've always wanted to be kissed like this. It's every girl's dream to be kissed like the other person can't get enough of you. It's only fair if I kiss him back just as hard and make him think I want this. Adrian can think whatever he wants about me. He can think I hate him. He can think I'm melting for him.

If I'm going to do this, I'm going to take as much as I give.

All I care about is the way it's going to feel when he takes control of all the heat between my legs. Will he kiss me there too? Will he be just as ravenous as he is now?

He kisses me harder, demanding more with a rumble from deep in his chest when he puts his hand on one of my legs and slides it slowly up under my dress. There's no hesitation at all with this movement. He got all he wanted from me when I told him I wasn't leaving. Now I'm his to take.

He pauses there before breaking our kiss and letting me breathe, his hand gripping my upper thigh. It's only then that I feel his cock pressed against my leg. He's hard and I wasn't mistaken earlier ... no wonder he's so fucking arrogant.

I shiver when he reaches my panties. They're not full coverage ones, because those don't sit well underneath my work clothes, but they're not a thong, either. His fingertips play at the band. Then he cups me through the cotton fabric and I moan into the kiss.

"You're hot for me," he says into my mouth. "I knew you would be the second you started to mouth off to me." Adrian strokes against the fabric and when his knuckles brush against my clit I'm all too aware of how sensitive I am for him. My head lolls to the side and I sink my teeth into the fabric of his shirt. My hands fist his dress shirt, pulling it from his suit pants with a desperate need for it to be ripped from him so we can get on with it.

"Good girl. Such a good little slut for me." My back arches and I rock myself into his hand. "Fuck you," I mutter but even as I do, the pleasure builds and Adrian chuckles. He's playing me like a toy.

The words make me hot even though I know they shouldn't. I roll my hips against his hand and he groans a deep rough sound, wrapping his other hand around the nape of my neck to pull me in close.

"Do you want to be my whore or my good girl?" he asks me.

I can only gasp as his fingers slip past the band and his thumb rubs ruthless circles against my clit. Moaning, I don't answer him.

"Degradation or praise?" he presses further.

I have both hands on his chest, slid under the expensive fabric of his shirt. "Whatever you want. I just need you inside of me." The plea is desperate, and I don't give a fuck.

He doesn't say a word as he smiles down at me like he's

won. For a half second, I worry he'll leave me like this, wanting and admitting it so boldly. The fear is gone just as quickly as it came. His hands go under my ass and he roughly lifts me onto the surface of his desk. Adrian uses one hand to push my legs apart and I balance myself on the desk while he shoves the hem of my dress up to my hips. The fabric rolls up in an awkward bunch and remains there. This dress isn't meant to be treated like that, but he doesn't care. He's busy pulling my panties off and down over my shoes, which fall to the floor with dull thuds. Finally, his fingertips meet my bare, wet center.

It turns me into a woman I don't know. A woman who five minutes ago was coming in here to tell him to keep his hands off my department. Now I'm so hungry for his touch that I practically throw myself into it. Adrian doesn't allow it. He takes what he wants, and he pushes me away from him, one hand splayed across my chest while reaching for his belt buckle with the other. His cock springs out with a flash of lust in his eyes. "Spread wide, Suzette."

I obey and he pulls my hips closer to the edge.

His eyes sweep down to my spread legs and he groans, his hand working at his cock. He wants the same thing from me that I want from him. He wants to work off some of the tension from endless meetings and boardrooms and constantly working, constantly holding everything in.

With a hand on the back of my head, he bends low to kiss me as he nudges the tip right where I need him. Adrian isn't taking time to make sure I'm ready and he doesn't have to. I'm more than ready for him. He pumps his hips and I hang on to the desk to stay on it.

Fuck! He fills me with a single hard thrust, his hand coming down to brace my ass so he can fuck me deeper. My hands fly to his shoulders, needing to hold on to something more solid. My body's hot all at once and tense. My heels dig into his ass.

"Fuck," I moan. Not slowing down in the least, Adrian's lips find mine again. "Fucking perfect," he groans. I bury my head into his chest, my eyes closing and my teeth biting down on my lip as he fucks me like he owns me. He whispers, "Take it like a good girl."

A cold sweat covers my forehead as I pull away, stifling my moans as best I can.

It's dirty to do this and so wrong. It's against every rule of office life to spread your legs on a man's desk ... especially when he's your boss. And certainly when he's your boss's boss. My body doesn't care. It clenches around him, making him grunt, and his lips capture my screams of pleasure. My release builds and rises like the tides on the shore until it's crashing down on me. The only option I'm left with is to hang on for dear life.

CHAPTER 3

ADRIAN

No matter how much she tries to hide it, I can still hear her catching her breath.

Fuck, it's hard enough to keep steady myself. My muscles are still coiled with adrenaline rushing through my veins. That was exactly what I needed.

With a hushed moan slipping through her lips as I button up my shirt, I amend the thought: *She* is exactly what I needed.

With my back turned to her, a satisfied smile creeps to my lips and I bend down to pick up my tie. "Do you have plans for dinner?" I ask, balling up the silk and pocketing it rather than attempting a professional appearance in the least.

The unmistakable sound of a zipper replaces the silence

in the room, as do the muffled sounds of her attempting to slip her heels back on. I turn to see her peering up at me.

Fuck.

There are so many questions that dance in her gorgeous light blue eyes. The vulnerability is unexpected. Her red dress is still open in the back; her attempt to zip it up only moved it partway.

Distrust riddles itself in every small movement she makes. It's so damn obvious as she stares back at me like she's afraid to even breathe.

"Turn around," I command her, not liking wherever her pretty little head has taken her. "Let me help you with that."

She only hesitates a moment, still not having answered my question. I take my time, using the backs of my fingers to brush her brunette locks to the side. My hand brushes against her bare back before I zip up her dress to the top. I don't miss that she uses her right hand to brace herself on the desk and she stares down at it rather than looking back at me. The obvious insecurity has my dick hardening already. If she thinks I only wanted her once or that this was some kind of manipulation tactic, my little vixen is dead wrong.

"I have reservations for dinner. Come with me."

She's silent still as she comes back to reality. Her cheeks are still flushed, her lips still swollen from my bruising kiss. With her hair disheveled, she looks well and thoroughly fucked.

Stepping to her right so as not to be trapped between myself and the desk I've just fucked her on, she leaves me wanting.

"I should go," is all she says.

Panic is something I didn't expect to feel. Certainly not with a woman like her, confident and transparent. If she leaves right now, I'm fucked. We barely spoke. There's no chance in hell she'll let me near her again.

This is not at all the way it was supposed to go.

"We have reservations and we're going to be late."

"We? *We* have reservations?" she says and finally looks me in the eye. That's better. Wherever her head is, whoever screwed her over to the point of not trusting another man, it's in the past.

"I don't want to go alone. So yes. We have reservations at the Waldorf."

"I'm not dressed for that," she responds far too quickly.

I make a point of letting my eyes undress her from head to toe. "The hell you aren't. You look utterly delectable."

"I would never wear something like this to the Waldorf."

Watching as she smooths her hair, her gaze dancing between me and the door, I offer her a simple solution. "We can stop on the way."

She rolls her eyes and my cock answers in response, hardening and wanting so desperately to punish her. "I have plenty of money if I—"

"I could buy you a thousand times over." My voice is harder than I'd like but I'm through with this little back-and-forth. "If I say we can stop to buy you whatever the hell I want, it's not because I wish to spoil you or show off. It's to save time and for your comfort."

My statement must have come off harsh, because her jaw clenches. I add, "I couldn't care less what you wear."

"I wouldn't want to be seen with someone like you, showing off your recent conquest." The bitterness to her tone might as well slap me across my face.

Is that what she thinks this is? Is that who she thinks I am?

Invading her space, I tower over her and say, "When did I give you the impression you were something to conquer? I want you because I want you, and I couldn't care less what anyone else thinks of that."

All that anger, all that resentment—it all vanishes the second I exert any dominance over her. It's addictive. It's heaven and hell, a concoction I'd gladly get drunk on every second for the rest of my life.

"I am one thing in the boardroom. I'm another outside of that. If you can't compartmentalize, tell me now."

"I'm sorry," she says and her doe eyes fall to my chest. She's on the verge of running and that's the last thing I want.

"I don't want you to apologize," I say, gentling my voice, tipping up her chin so she'll finally look at me. See me. "I want you to come to dinner with me."

CHAPTER 4

SUZETTE

What the fuck just happened?

I'm not certain how I made it downstairs from his office with his hand splayed across my lower back, in front of anyone who dared to look. My legs are weak and there's an odd mix of satisfaction and nervousness that has my head clouded.

Adrian Bradford just fucked me across his desk like I was his personal toy. The feel of him between my legs is all I can focus on. How effortlessly he destroyed every wall I've built and fucked me like he had every right in the world to ruin me.

I'm barely with it as he helps me to his car until he speaks to his driver, who politely greets me before opening the back door. Adrian says something to him that I don't quite make out because I'm still catching my breath from the sex.

The cool spring air brings me back to the present as I thank his driver. He's an older gentleman with a lean frame and silver hair. His wire-rimmed glasses and black suit complete his polished look.

"Thank you," I say, barely getting out the words before I'm left alone in the back of the car, until Adrian climbs in on his side.

It's a Mercedes, one of the new ones from this year, and it smells like he just drove it off the lot. Adrian's driver rolls up the divider that separates the spacious back seat from the front the moment he gets in.

Adrian sprawls out on the seat next to me as the driver navigates the city streets. He's on his phone like nothing happened and I try to act like nothing happened too. I'm having a bit of trouble with that. He seems casual, swiping at the screen and no doubt answering emails, but there's tension crackling between us. No matter how hard he tries to make this into nothing, it's anything but.

Gaining a semblance of balance and sanity, I peer up at him and say, as clearly as I can, "I'm not a toy to be played with."

He glances at me, then slips his phone into his back pocket. "You seemed to enjoy it quite a bit."

My face reddens. "I did. But that doesn't mean it can continue or that my job ..." my voice trails off and I can barely swallow. *What the fuck did I just do?*

He studies me with his pale blue gaze. "Would you like it, though?" There's far too much space between us in the back seat of his car. Adrian's taking care not to touch me. It feels deliberate. He doesn't move his body toward me or reach for me, but I can still feel his hands on me from just a moment ago. I can feel where he gripped my ass and held me close for a kiss by my neck, and where he stroked between my legs. "Would you like it if I toyed with you again?" he asks, his voice low and his words sinful.

The rest of my body feels as hot as my face. Now that we're out of the office and away from the moment, I can't believe it happened. What was I thinking? I can't answer him, because I'm not sure of myself enough to speak. It's all too much and far too fast. Suffocating.

"I'd like an answer, Suzette," he says and his murmur is laced with something different. Concern.

Swallowing thickly, I admit, "I enjoyed it very much, but now—"

"I enjoyed it immensely and I intend to toy with you, to fuck you until you're as limp as a little ragdoll, and to walk back into the office tomorrow knowing full damn well you may give me hell."

The leather groans in protest as he leans back, moving farther away as he studies me. "Nothing that just happened will interfere with our work," he reassures me.

With a jostle of the vehicle, the driver pulls the car to

the curb, and I blink at the scenery outside my window. The Waldorf, another public arena for his games ... and a far too expensive one at that. I murmur, "You should take me home."

He's silent for a moment, just watching me. "If that's what you'd like. I believe I owe you more than just a drink, though, Suzette."

Hearing my name from his lips like that ... like every syllable rolls off his tongue as if he was the first to utter them, turns me even hotter. It also makes me speechless, which isn't like me at all. None of this is like me at all. I don't get swept up into anything.

Adrian holds me in place with his piercing gaze. "I'd very much like to play with you, Suzette. I'd like to kiss you. I'd like to fuck you. And not just because you're a pretty little thing who stormed into my office making demands you have no authority to make."

With every word, he inches closer to me until he's close enough to kiss me. The proximity is comforting in a way I don't care to admit. Adrian actually leans down and does it. He kisses me full on the mouth, his lips steady and confident. When he pulls back I have to keep my hands in my lap from grabbing his shirt.

"It was a brutal day, and the only thing that kept me grounded and kept me looking forward to tonight was the very idea that you were coming to my office to do exactly what you did." His admission shocks me.

"Adrian ..."

"You may see me as ruthless and heartless, and you may not like what I do, but I'd like to see you again. In and out of the office."

It's strange for him to admit this to me. Most men won't ever acknowledge they're aware of other people's feelings. Men like Adrian aren't supposed to care what anyone else thinks. It's possible he doesn't care, but at least he's aware of it. It causes a shift in the way I see him. The hatred softens and becomes something else.

"When the workday is over, there are other things we must do. And then there are things that we *want* to do." He leans in closer, whispering at the shell of my ear, "I want you."

His hand comes down on my knee and without hesitation he pushes it up between my legs, forcing my skirt up as his fingers brush against my slit. It's the softest of touches and my eyes close, my lips parted and my head falling back. Adrian lets out a groan, the tip of his nose running along my neck, teasing me. "You didn't put your panties back on."

I shake my head, unable to speak. I didn't. I tucked them into my purse, not liking their condition after ... well, after what he did to me. Adrian dips his head again, close enough to kiss, and I want it so much that tears come to my eyes. I'm not even sure what they mean. Adrian seems to know.

"You," he says, "are exactly what I want."

He takes a deep breath and then exhales, the warmth

of it lingering as he pulls away slightly. Trapped in his car, every sensation feels heightened, knowing how easy it is for him to admit his desire. I become aware of his hands. One holds the seat behind me, just above my head, and the one that was between my legs is now braced against the door, like he must hold on to something to keep him from touching me. From doing whatever it is he so desperately craves to do. Adrian's eyes close for a moment and when he opens them, he seems steadier than before. "If you'd like to go home, I'll take you home. I'll have my driver take you wherever you need. Though I'd very much like to take you to dinner."

"I'm not dressed for this place."

"We could go somewhere else."

"You have reservations," I say and my pulse races, not wanting me to deny him … or myself.

"That's a weak excuse, Suzette." Disappointment flashes across his face, and surprise grips my heart. I'm surprised I care about his disappointment and I'm even more shocked that I *want* to go to dinner with him. He feels dangerous, like he could crush me if he wanted. Yet I find myself wanting to be under his thumb, wondering what he'll do to me.

I don't know where I'm supposed to draw the line, though. This is … this is something that could certainly destroy me, and then what would I have left?

I imagine how it will feel to have the car pull away from the curb and drop me at my place. And then I imagine what it would be like to let him help me out of the car and take me inside this restaurant. Both options leave me wanting, but only one feels safe.

"Is it a business dinner?" I ask, keeping my voice low and even.

A grin tugs the corners of his mouth upward. "No. It's after six."

"If someone asks?" A bit of desperation creeps into my tone, and I can't stop it. "Could it be a business dinner if someone were to see us?"

"You'd like to be discreet?"

I have to be discreet. I don't even know what this is. A hate fuck turned into a dinner date? There's no telling what I might want to keep hidden later.

"Yes," I answer. "Please. It would make me feel better."

He seems to consider it, searching my expression as we sit in the back of the parked car. "Would you like to see me again after tonight?"

There's a pressure in my chest, like a balloon getting filled up with helium. It reminds me of the excitement I felt when I was young and dumb and dating. Before I got married and everything went to shit. There was a period in my life when it seemed like anything could happen. That woman would revel in this moment. But that woman got her heart ripped out long ago. She's long dead and buried.

"It depends," I finally make myself say. "On how our

discreet dinner goes."

Adrian smirks, charming and seductive, making him all the more handsome. It sends a shiver of desire down my spine. I already want him again. Even at this point there's so much heat between us and it seems impossible to turn it down. Above all, I want to see him smile at me with approval. I've never been a people pleaser. I've always been about making change, and change is often uncomfortable for others. Part of me still wants to *please* him. *I want to hear him call me his good girl again.*

"So you'll come to dinner with me and then decide? That's a fair deal."

Adrian stares at me across the table of our rather private curved booth. His gaze is fire; everything about him is possessive, but in a manner that's effortless. Every little thing, including the way his touch never left me when he escorted me into the Waldorf, is dominating yet in a way that's gentle. I could have walked faster or simply pulled away from him, but there was never a moment where I considered such a betrayal. Both to what he obviously desires, as well as my own.

Tucked away in the corner of the restaurant, with fine leather upholstery covering the padded wooden frame, it's easy enough to peek out at the other guests, although they feel miles away. It feels like they're all staring at us, though they're not. I shift in my seat. If they're looking over here, they'll notice I'm underdressed.

"I love seeing you squirm," says Adrian in a low voice.

"About the meeting today ..." I begin.

"We're off the clock," he says simply, ending the conversation without breaking my gaze.

I bite my lip and try to keep from bringing up work again. It would be so easy to fall into that.

The tension is still there, and I do my best to not so nervously lay the napkin across my lap as the waiter presents the menu to us.

I let the menu fall as Adrian orders for me. He's quick and confident, as if we already know each other.

"Would that be all right?" he asks and inclines his head toward me before the waiter can leave. Nodding, I give my seal of approval.

I wait until the waiter has stepped out of earshot before I speak to him. "You're lucky you chose what you did."

"I guessed right? Or are you just saying that?" His eyes on mine seem to see right through my dress, as if he's remembering earlier at the office.

"You did guess right." My fingers slip along the stem of my water goblet.

"If it's not to your liking, I'll have them bring you something else," he says, and I feel myself blushing with a sudden shyness I haven't felt in years. Not since I was a girl. There's no place for shyness in a business career like mine. Adrian puts a hand to my face and runs his thumb over my cheek.

"You get to me, Adrian."

"That seems fair, since you get to me as well." Butterflies stir and I can't help it. "Are you always like this?" I question but all I'm rewarded with is a charming, knowing smirk before we're interrupted.

The waiter reappears, and there's distance between us again. In his starched black uniform, the waiter sets out a wineglass. Then he shows Adrian the bottle, and at Adrian's nod he opens it and pours a sip or two. Adrian tastes it. The waiter watches him the same way I'm watching him. Probably too closely. He lets the wine linger on his tongue before swallowing it and giving the waiter a nod.

He fills my glass and places it in front of me, murmuring his replies to our thank-yous, and Adrian curls his fist around his own glass. Whiskey, on the rocks.

I watch him take the first sip and notice the way his shoulders relax.

"Is this how you are with all your employees?" I ask.

Adrian raises an eyebrow. "I haven't slept with an employee ever, actually."

"Why do I find that hard to believe?" I arch an eyebrow, leaning in, trying to flirt with him.

He answers me in an utterly serious tone. "Because you

don't trust me and seem to hold a rather low opinion of me."

I jerk back a few inches, shock settling in. Is he really offended by this? We just had sex on his desk, in his office, at work. The only boundary was that it was slightly after 6:00 p.m. "I didn't mean to imply that I think poorly of you. And for the record, it's because you exude sex appeal so I imagine you could sleep with anyone you wanted."

Adrian chuckles, his rough short laugh a baritone rumble in his chest, and it breaks up the tension. "You do seem very hesitant around me. Is there something I can do to ease that?" His words fall slowly, drifting to the pressed and starched linen tablecloth as his eyes drop to my breasts. "To break the ice, perhaps?"

"You have a reputation, Adrian."

"Everyone does, Suzette. It doesn't mean that's who we are. One person could tell you I'm loyal to a fault, another that I'm a miserable asshole. Both could very well be honest impressions of me. So, believe them both."

Before I can even respond, we're interrupted yet again.

"Excuse me, sir." The waiter steps to the side of the table and passes a folded note to Adrian.

With Adrian's nod we're alone again, although I might as well not exist.

He reads it, tucks the thick white note card into his pocket, and checks his phone.

My stomach drops. "Is everything all right?"

His phone goes back into his pocket. "As all right as it always is."

My teeth sink into my bottom lip as I gather my courage for the next question, which I should have asked before I fucked him. "There isn't another woman, is there?"

"No." The answer comes quickly and decisively, and I believe him. "I haven't had a sexual partner for the better part of a year."

The handle of my fork rests in my fingertips, but I drop it back down to the empty small plate again. "No other man?" he questions in turn.

"No." It's a relief to hear that. A bigger relief than I would have thought.

"And we're to be discreet?" Adrian finishes.

"Yes," I say.

"Work during the day, and play at night?"

"Yes," I answer.

His eyes narrow. "I like when you answer me like that, a single word rushing out of your perfect, parted lips." His gaze burns. "I'd like to see those lips when I—"

Adrian gets another text and curses under his breath. He's not the only one. My phone buzzes too.

It's from Maddie: *Hey! Are you coming?*

"Oh ... I'm so sorry." I push my hair back from my face and brace myself with both hands on the table. "I'm supposed to meet a friend tonight. I completely forgot."

Of the three women I'm closest to, Maddie is like my little sister. She's also going through a breakup and relying heavily on company to keep her from texting the asshole when she feels lonely.

"I can't believe I forgot."

"No time to eat?" he questions, not pressuring me in the least. His phone buzzes yet again before I can even answer, and he closes his eyes, visibly annoyed.

"I'm sorry, I really have to go. She's a good friend of mine and I don't know how it could have possibly slipped my mind that we had plans." I swallow down the horrible feeling of failing her, knowing exactly how I came to forget about anything other than the man seated in front of me. "I'm going to take a cab."

"If you insist."

"I'm afraid I do, Mr. Bradford." As I speak, I stand and he mirrors the motion.

"No longer Adrian?"

He holds his hand out to me and it takes me a minute to understand what he wants. "I'll walk you out."

It's almost unreal what a gentleman this man is after hours. "Will you be so kind to me tomorrow?" I question as if it's banter, but the truth is obviously buried there.

It only takes one motion from Adrian for the doorman to bring around a taxi for me. The night has fallen dark and the chill brings me closer to Adrian as the car pulls up.

"Phone." He says the one word and I hand him my phone without question. Adrian frowns down at the screen while he types something. It's his number. His fingers fly across the screen. I'll probably find out he's sent a text to himself with my number.

"I'll see you tomorrow," he says, handing it back to me. "Perhaps you'll give me the opportunity to play with you once the clock strikes six."

Chapter 5

Adrian

It takes great effort not to let on that my pants are tight from my little vixen's text messages. I'm certain Wyatt wouldn't appreciate that fact.

With that being said, it's my office. My meeting.

And if I want to read the filthy things she's messaging, I'll damn well do as I please.

I'll have to scold her when I see her. Not now, while she's working, when I'm not buried deep inside her and she has nowhere to go.

Scrolling through the last messages she sent, I have to readjust in my seat.

Suzette Parks has a very dirty mouth and I want to do

very dirty things to it.

It's work hours, though, so I don't respond to the three she's sent me.

This morning was one thing, and technically I started the "sexting games" as she called it.

No panties today. I want to fuck you without having to rip them off.

Yes, sir.

That's my good girl.

You say that now but if you tell me to crawl under your desk, that will be a firm no from me.

Why do I think you're lying?

I remember when I sent the last message, I watched both the clock and the security monitors that kept track of her entering the elevator. It was nearly 9:00 a.m.

Tell me what you would do then, if I wanted you to keep me company in my office.

Did I set her up? Fucking right I did. Am I going to fuck her hard and rough to punish her for the unprofessional behavior she's displayed? Hell yes I am. And we're both going to enjoy it.

It's all talk from her. I know it is. So, scolding her will have to wait.

"I don't know, man," Wyatt says, nudging the container of lo mein closer to me. Piling the bit of it left on his plate onto a white plastic fork he tells me, "I prefer the place on Fifth."

"Shing Kwong?"

He nods, still shoveling the Chinese food into his mouth. Wyatt is tall, lean, and three years younger than me although it feels like there's a decade between us. He's naive, positive about far too much and riskier than he should be.

I didn't come from money. We were slightly well-off, but not like the Pattons, Wyatt's family. It shows. He makes deals like there will always be a safety net beneath him. I'd be lying if I said I wasn't resentful of it at one time in my life. As the end of a noodle slaps his chin, sauce dripping down his amber skin, the corners of my lips turn up.

Wyatt is a puppy dog in the elite groups I run in, but he's damn loyal.

"Yeah."

"Well, you're welcome to bring your own takeout next time you decide to swing by then, rather than having Andrea order it."

"So I'll have that contract for you in just a little bit."

My brow arches at the very sudden change in topics. "I knew you'd bring it up."

He smirks, not looking back at me, and says, "I can't help it; I'm excited."

"I haven't said I'll sign, and I'm still waiting on my lawyer to look over the clauses."

"It's been a year in the making," he comments, finally putting down his plate.

"I'm not sure it's the right time right now."

It's silent for a moment and Wyatt finally looks up at me,

running his hand over his curly, jet-black hair. It's cropped close to his scalp with a slight fade on the sides. "'Cause of this," he says and motions behind him with his thumb.

Because of the eight-figure company I just bought? Yes. That would be why. Although I'd never admit it out loud. My funds aren't typically tied up in so many holdings. The timing was right for Holt & Hanover, though. He was desperate and I had the last bit of cash flow I could manage.

"You know I don't go into these things lightly."

One thick black brow raises as he leans back in the chair, pointing a finger at me. "You know this is a good deal."

"It *could* be a good deal," I respond, correcting him and before he can say any more, I tell him, "Let the lawyers talk out the details."

"They're minor," he presses, his insecurity showing as he grips the armrest of the lounge chair. "The merger is going to be a hit and I know you want in on it."

I mirror his posture, leaning back in my seat as I ball up my napkin and toss it onto my empty paper plate that's stained from lunch. "A number of events need to go accordingly." In this business, there are ebbs and flows. Some people can't handle the wild swings. Some don't prepare for the crashes.

"You sound like my father," Wyatt quips.

I merely grunt, checking my phone again and see she hasn't messaged any more. I'm tempted to send another text regardless. My thumb taps on the desk, my attention very much focused on the last line she sent an hour ago.

"Who is she?" he asks and I stare back at him blankly.

"Of all the—" Just as a grin stretches across his face, ready to lay into me, there's a knock at the door.

"Come in." I'm grateful for the interruption.

"Mr. Bradford," Andrea says, stepping into the room. If it weren't for the faint wrinkles around her eyes and the corners of her mouth, she'd look two decades younger than she is.

"Andrea could look it over?" Wyatt suggests and then huffs a laugh.

"She looks over all my contracts," I'm quick to tell him. She may only hold the title of secretary, and she looks the part, but Andrea Anderson is sharp and has a legal background that could rival the best. Times were different back then and instead of a firm, or the head of an academic department, Andrea left law altogether and I was lucky enough to meet her before someone else got ahold of her.

"Sir." Andrea folds her hands in front of her pencil skirt. "Your one o'clock is seated in the conference room."

All traces of humor are gone and dread seeps in.

"Thank you, Andrea." As I stand, Wyatt watches me button my jacket and take a mint.

Everything feels stiff and uncomfortable.

The moment the door closes gently, Andrea disappearing behind it, Wyatt comments, "Uh-oh. I'm guessing someone is about to get a harsh scolding from their new CEO."

I huff a humorless laugh, striding around him and tossing what's left of lunch into the trash.

"Can you clean up on your way out?"

"Yeah, you all right?" he questions as I open the door and glance through to the conference room. There's a reason there's only one office up here and then that room.

I get a glimpse of some of the employees seated around a table, my hand still on the doorknob. My hand is clenched so tight, my knuckles have gone white.

"You going to fire someone?" Wyatt makes another guess and this time he's right. I look over my shoulder to inform him, "An entire department. A very inefficient, very much *unneeded* department." I feel sick to my stomach just saying it. Knowing how in a single meeting I'll change their lives forever. But it's the right decision. The company is bleeding money with these cookie-cutter executives. Their pay increased while tasks were delegated and as the company grew, their roles diminished as new employees took on tasks that came with new demands. A dozen men and women walked into this building today overlooking tasks they barely comprehend.

"Shit," Wyatt says and he doesn't hold back on the misery. "I know if you're doing it, it must be done." His large brown eyes look sympathetic.

"Tell that to them."

CHAPTER 6

SUZETTE

Adrian is most of the reason I couldn't sleep. Those dreams were too hot to forget and they made me twist and turn in the sheets until morning. There was plenty to keep my mind occupied between replaying what happened on his office desk and the way he treated me after. The man himself is a whirlwind and I can barely hold on. There's an ache between my thighs still, even though it's been hours and hours.

The tall macchiato does nothing to help the bags under my eyes, but with a deep breath in, I prepare to make my way to my office like nothing happened.

Stepping foot inside feels illicit in a way it never did before. I've always come in with my chin up, ready to do battle for another day. Today that kick-ass persona is nowhere to be found. It's somewhere between a childish puppy dog love and the feelings that accompany the walk of shame.

In all those hours of tossing and turning, I came to one conclusion: I have, what feels like, a crush. Back in high school I used to get this fluttering-heart feeling for some of the guys in my class ... that ended less than well. Pining after men in college led to my ex-husband. So all of these feelings can fuck off. It's against everything I stand for to have that kind of feeling for Adrian. It's forbidden to have sex with your boss on his desk. It's wrong to daydream about it so much you lose focus on your work.

It's a no go. A hard pass. But I'll be damned if I didn't text him the second he messaged me. Those giddy little feelings are my kryptonite. I suppose there's always an exception to every rule and Adrian Bradford is just that: exempt from every boundary I've spent years defining. Even as I sit at my desk, the tapping of keys and hushed chatter around me, I can barely keep from looking toward the elevator. All I want to know is if he's up there. I want to know if he can't stop thinking about what happened on his desk either.

Hours pass slowly through the day until I get a text message from him at four. His name on my phone makes the temperature of my body kick up a notch. I swallow hard, trying to subdue it all.

Adrian: *Meet me at the elevator at six.*

The hours went by slowly before but now they drag on and on, each tick of the clock taking forever. I stare at my computer screen, rereading every email twice. Triple-checking my responses to clients and sending back nearly every design I'm given from the graphics department. Not because they need changing or that they don't fit the branding for said clients. But simply because I can't focus and there's no way in hell I'm approving anything when all I keep imagining is my boss's expression when he calls me good girl.

At four fifteen there's a meeting in one of the smaller conference rooms downstairs. It's all I can do not to stare at Adrian through the large paned windows. In the glances I do steal, he appears less than thrilled. Every expression is dour as they leave one by one, Adrian leaving last and not looking back.

At ten to five, half a dozen executive assistants and senior executive assistants, some of whom I know but most I don't, move through the office in a clump. It's a relief that something has happened to break up the routine of the day.

"Fired," Gail whispers to me. I nearly spill my coffee when she does. I didn't realize she was standing so close, also spying.

"What?" I question. I've known Gail for years now. She's a damn good resource for client retention, but also the lead watercooler gossip. "Did you say fired? Are you sure?"

Nodding, she sweeps her curly dark brown hair back over one shoulder and then holds her coffee cup with both hands.

In heels and leaning against the wall, the modelesque Latina in her late twenties towers over me. "I bet there will be an email going out soon."

All of them? Fired? She leaves me with a sick feeling stirring in the pit of my stomach as she bids her farewell. "It's what he does. No one should be surprised."

I know he has a reputation, but how the hell can a company run if every executive is severed?

Not long after that, an assistant director, Daniel Prath, who I spotted in the conference room earlier, has a screaming fit at the elevators with another man I don't know. Including the phrases, "this company would have gone under without me" and "good luck staying in business."

They must be fired, then.

Although the whispers that spread, in part largely to Gail, include fears of the company running with so many leads laid off at once, most don't mind seeing them leave. I'm certain a few who were under the executive assistant in finance will cheer in celebration to that prick's departure. All I ever heard about him were complaints.

It doesn't take more than an hour to pass before there's a conclusion among the majority of whispers: Those men encompass all that is wrong with the corporate world. They let people go rather than compensating them in the manner they should have been paid. They hired new employees and paid them less, pushing more onto everyone else's plate. They demanded more and more from all of us, wanting everyone to take one for the team while increasing their bonuses every year.

It's not good for a business to run that way, and it's not good for people to live that way. The management here uses up employees until they break, then fires them and starts over. They've never acknowledged or paid their respects to the employees who made the company what it is.

And now they're walking out the door.

Five o'clock comes and nearly everyone is gone already. Most taking the day off to "readjust" to new procedures from their higher-ups. I stay, like I always do. The last hour, when everyone's left and it's quiet, when the emails stop and calls go to voicemail, are my most productive. Judging by Adrian's statement yesterday, and his message from today, six is when the clock strikes midnight for him as well.

Somehow, that makes those giddy, girly feelings all the headier.

It's six on the dot when I press the silver button with the arrow icon pointing downward for the elevator. I don't know how I'm able to stand upright, with the nervousness that runs through me.

It isn't like me, none of this is. But I'd be lying if I said it wasn't thrilling.

When the doors open, my heart races at the sight in front of me. Adrian is already there waiting for me. Forcing myself to move slowly so he doesn't see my anxiousness, I move to his side and turn to face the doors. "I expect there will be a company-wide email shortly," I say to him as if it's casual conversation. We both stare straight ahead, the doors still open, making each second pass by at an achingly slow rate.

"Why is that?" He moves to press the button for the foyer and I note the way his bespoke suit wraps around his broad shoulders. And the way he fills the not-so-small cabin with his presence alone.

"I hear heads will be rolling."

As the elevator door closes, he smirks at me, a devilish look that brings an overwhelming heat to my cheeks. The elevator begins its descent and he asks, "Is that the talk at the watercooler?"

"More like the profanity Prath screamed on his way out."

He chuckles, then reaches for the button again. One strong knuckle pushes in the emergency stop button.

Tick, tick, tick, my heart rages in my chest. Desire fills me, moving over my skin and pinning me in place. I should know better than to do this but I don't. He's a fantasy come to life and I won't deny myself. How could a lowly sinner say no when the devil himself tempts her?

Confined in a small space together with no way out unless he decides and presses that button ... all I feel is want and desire.

With one decisive stride, Adrian towers over me and personal space is nonexistent. My heel slips back half a step before I think better of it. He was calm and collected when I stepped onto the elevator, but now his eyes burn with a hunger I know all too well. With my next breath, the scent of his cologne fills my lungs.

"I've had a rather difficult day," he rasps. "And it's well after six p.m."

He pushes me against the wall all at once and it's just like when he put me on top of his desk. Reasoning becomes impossible and pushing him away is even more unlikely. Adrian slides my dress up, his hands hot and his touch sending every nerve ending beneath it into flames.

His hands roam in every place I've thought of him touching, of him claiming, since I left him last night. He's rough and commanding, gripping my curves and devouring my neck with openmouthed kisses. Every sensation is ignited and all I can do is hold on. With my arms around his shoulders, I can barely breathe, the heat suffocating me.

I don't doubt he's missed this as much as I have. Maybe he did spend his day like I did, obsessed with the idea of continuing what we started yesterday.

With ease he spreads my legs, standing between them and undoes his buckle. My back is pressed against the hard metal. I hook my knee around his hip and drop my head back against the elevator wall. "Suzette," he growls against my neck. It's even hotter now in the small space, because of how much I want him and because of the need in his voice.

He strokes his fingers between my legs, teasing me and I can barely stand it. "You were hot and bothered all night, weren't you?" he says, his piercing gaze staring deep into mine. He smirks while he asks the question, confident that he's right.

"No, I barely thought of you."

He chuckles at my response and then calls me a liar as two of his thick fingers push inside of me. "Tell me how much you want me."

"I want you," I moan, and rock as much as I can to feel more of him inside of me.

When he tsks, stilling his motions, I open my eyes. "Uh, uh, uh. If you're going to move your hips like that, it won't be for anything but me."

He takes his cock in his fist and lines it up with my wet slit, then thrusts in. The movement is so hard and controlling that it takes my breath away. I gasp at the size of him and he pauses, buried deep inside of me, as I adjust to his girth.

"That's my good girl," he says in a breathy voice against my neck. It doesn't take long for him to move again, and I meet him with every thrust, my heels digging into his ass.

"Yes," he coaxes. "You have no fucking idea how hot you are," he groans, pulling a strap of my dress down and kissing, nipping down my shoulder to my breast.

My voice deserts me and I can't reply other than to angle my hips to take him deeper. My nails scratch at his jacket, in an effort to hold on to him.

It's fast. It's dirty. And I want to remember every last detail.

The elevator door dings. I'm still trying to get my breathing to a normal rate, but at least my hair doesn't give anything away. My dress is as smooth as it can be, but there's no doubt that I'm a hue pinker than I ought to be given that the city has a chill in the air this late in April.

As I walk with him, keeping pace, I remind myself there are no obligations. This is nothing but a fling, or an office fuck buddy. Given that I haven't dated in the better part of a decade other than the one-night stands I had to celebrate leaving my piece of shit ex, I have no idea what we are.

But I want more of it.

The thought of whatever we are is both exciting and terrifying. Adrian makes me feel things, but I'm smart enough not to fall for him. I have to be, or this could end very badly. Hands to my hair, I smooth it down one more time and prepare to tell him a quick good night. My heels click on the marble floor of the lobby and I note that the place is nearly vacant. But not entirely. No one looks our way, though. I thank my lucky stars for that.

As we get to the large glass doors that lead to the bustling streets, I start what I think will be an acceptable farewell, "That was—"

"Come with me tonight." He's firm, businesslike as he stands toe to toe with me, waiting for an answer. His words reverberate through me, cutting off the farewell in addition to my thoughts.

"You don't need to buy me dinner."

"Do you eat?" he questions and there's not a trace of humor.

"Yes."

"Good." His eyes glint. "I want to feed you. Besides, we have things to discuss and we have—"

"You've made decisions regarding my department?" I question him, the sight from this afternoon putting me on edge instantly. "The only thing I've received from your team is a request for the client list."

That list is as good as gold. Everything they wanted in that email was essentially preparing paperwork so that another person could take over if need be. I'm not stupid, but I am under contract and not the only one with the list.

"We won't be discussing work at dinner."

"I can damn well discuss what I'd like."

"Watch that mouth of yours." His mouth quirks but he doesn't quite smile. More of a smirk. "It's after six," he whispers, and with the look he gives me, I glance over my shoulder to be sure no one is watching.

Adrian fixes his cuffs, readjusting his sleeves. "I have a late meeting with an associate. His wife wanted to do a tour of New York on a private ship. You could accompany me.

The meeting will be short, and they're good company. I've heard the chef they hired for tonight is excellent as well."

The heat from the elevator is back, and all of it is on my face. "I thought we were just—"

"I want more than sex, Suzette. Although I enjoy that immensely."

"What exactly do you want, Mr. Bradford?"

"To get to know you," he says simply.

It throws me off. What we were doing in his office and the elevator is so forbidden that I'd assumed we would have strong boundaries and never cross them. Getting to know each other is definitely crossing them. "Well ... the first thing I typically tell someone is I'm divorced and I hate the male species."

The lift of his brow is telling: *I wasn't acting like I hated him in the elevator.* "Surely there is more to you than your dating status."

I hesitate. "I'm not looking for anything serious."

"Having dinner after sex is serious?"

"Hanging on your arm as a date to an after-hours event? Being seen together ... that's not discreet."

"I assure you, my evenings are discreet. Nearly everyone I speak to has signed an NDA with me at some point or another and it's all business."

"If you think you need to woo me or somehow ..." I can't finish. I don't know how to say what I'm thinking.

"Or what?"

I decide to be blunt. "I don't mind just being a fuck toy," I admit to him, my voice low. "In fact, I enjoy it."

He groans as if I said it just to torture him. "Your fucking mouth, Suzette."

He must know how hot he is when he does that. When he speaks to me like that. It's not fair in the least. I have to bite down on my lip to keep from grinning. A genuine smile, different from the one I use in meetings or when I pass people in the hall at work.

He straightens and runs a hand over his mouth. "I'll make this very simple for you. I'm attracted to you. I'd like you to come with me tonight. Now say yes."

I try to read his expression. Unsettled and hot, I search for the meaning behind his words and the meaning behind his intentions. More importantly, what they'll do to me.

"Don't make me beg, Suzette," he states as if he really would. "Come. Say yes."

I answer without thinking, "Yes."

CHAPTER 7

ADRIAN

Suzette's phone rings the moment she gets into the car and she chooses not to answer it, texting instead.

With a cocked brow, I glance at her phone and she shakes her head, her expression not hiding the humor. She holds up her phone and says, "My friend Maddie."

The texts read as follows:

Sorry, can't take the call, everything okay?

Fine. Any word on what Lucifer is planning to do?

Nothing yet.

Well come over and drink with me, we'll do a binge watch of Grey's or something.

I have to work.

Booooo. Well don't let Lucifer get you down.

"Lucifer?" I question, feeling the corners of my lips pull into a knowing smirk.

She clears her throat, crossing her legs in an attempt to look dignified. "When I heard Holt sold the company to some asshole with a reputation ... We nicknamed him Lucifer."

My smile grows. "Hmm, sounds like a prick."

She has the decency to appear nervous under my gaze.

"Why is she asking about the company?"

"I outsource to her at times. And I've been ... nervous and venting to her."

"You overthink things."

"I think them through as much as I need to, thank you for your concern, though," she responds with every ounce of the defiance I covet.

"Your smart mouth reminds me of something." My cock hardens as I pull out my phone and read her messages aloud.

"I'd like the wall first, fucking me midday so everyone could hear what you do to me." My tone is even as I read but when I pause, I make my desire obvious, readjusting in my seat. With a devilish grin I peek over at Suzette, finding her cheeks to be a scarlet red. A gruff chuckle escapes me as her lips part and her eyes widen.

"Adrian." The admonishment is hushed and it's only when her gaze darts to the front of the car that I understand why.

"Noah, would you put the divider up please," I call up to

him and within seconds the dark partition is in place, granting us more privacy.

"You're blushing as badly as I am," she teases, joy clearly peppered in the statement. I can feel the heat in my cheeks.

"I'm sure he didn't hear anything," I tell her, although ... I have no fucking clue. "He's signed a nondisclosure agreement," I add for good measure.

Before she can distract from the conversation anymore, I read the second text. "At night, I'd love for you to fuck me against the window, so I could feel the city beneath us and know every single one of them would trade places with us in a heartbeat." My words are spoken lowly, carefully but not in a whisper.

With her hands spearing through her hair that sits on her shoulders, she pulls the loose strands back as if she needs to feel the cool air against the back of her neck. "What?" she says and shrugs, her expression the picture-perfect resemblance of a minx.

"We have a work relationship during those hours, Ms Parks. I'm going to have to punish you for such ... foul language and indiscretion."

Her brow arches, although she plays along with me. "Should I not respond to you then from nine to six?"

"It depends," I answer, "do you want me to play with you in the car on the way to dinner or not?"

Her simper grows wider. "That depends. What exactly

do you have in mind for my punishment?"

Her chest rises with a heavy breath and her skin flushes as I unzip my pants and pull my cock through. At the sight of a bead of precum, Suzette licks her lower lip. I pat my lap. "Lay your head here and put your ass up on the seat so I can reach you."

Lying across the seat, her buckle still in place, she eagerly takes the head of my dick in her mouth, moaning and sending soft vibrations of lust to run through me.

I stifle the groan and press the intercom button for Noah. "Go round the block if we get there before I call up."

"Yes, sir," he answers back just in time for my little vixen to pull herself off my dick with a little pop. She works my length as she looks up at me, a perfect view of her breasts on full display.

"Back down, take your punishment like a good girl."

She asks breathlessly, her lips already reddened and slightly swollen, "This is my punishment?"

Smirking down at her, I take my time, pulling up her dress and feeling her bare pussy already wet. "My cock is to keep you quiet."

She eases herself back down my length and I palm one globe of her ass before squeezing it and then the other, warming her ass up.

"You're going to take my cock as far down your throat as you can," I tell her, lowering my lips to be closer to her ear. "And I'm going to toy with you, spank you, and bring you to the edge."

Her gorgeous blue eyes look up at me through her thick lashes and I swear it's the most beautiful sight I've ever seen. "Don't you dare bite me," I warn her before slapping my hand against her ass. It's enough that my palm stings, her mouth opens wider and my cock drives deeper into the back of her throat.

She doesn't choke, but she sputters. The sensation of my cock being pressed against the back of her throat feels like heaven.

My middle finger drops lower, playing between her folds as I wait for her to readjust. With my toes curled, and her mouth already bringing me close, I spank her ass again and again. Two quick strikes and she cries out, whimpering and pulling off my cock.

Thank fuck.

Barely containing myself, I tsk her as if she isn't doing everything perfectly. Everything is just as I want.

"Adrian," she pleads, but doesn't object, taking a moment to readjust, the leather groaning beneath us.

"You're doing well," I say and comfort her, rubbing soothing circles against her heated skin. With her lips putting pressure on the head of my cock, she works her way down again and I'm quick to decide on the punishment in my head. There's no fucking way I can get through ten of these. "Two more," I barely get out, the pleasure building.

I make them harder than the first two, and the slaps resonate in the small cabin.

She groans, her cheeks hollowing and her brow pinched until I massage the sensitized skin and then lean over more. With one hand splayed across her back, keeping her down, the other is in the perfect position to play with her pussy.

She jerks on my cock as I dip my middle finger inside her, curling it and finding that sweet spot. I know the moment I hit it because she writhes for me, unable to stay still.

Thank fuck. "I want to feel you come on my hand," I tell her and she mewls. She fucking mewls for me and then she moans my name as if she's already on edge.

I'm merciless as I finger fuck her, desperate for her to come before I do. She loses her composure, pulling off my cock and opting to pump me with her hand so she can breathe in short pants.

"Adrian." She says my name as if she's begging.

"Come for me. You're such a good fucking slut for me, taking whatever I give you."

"Oh my fuck," she says as her hands grip my thigh, her back arches and she cries out her pleasure into my suit pants, burying her head there and leaving my cock aching with need.

When she spasms around my fingers, I swear it takes all of me not to come undone with her.

"Good girl." The praise comes with deeper, calming breaths and she pushes herself up with chaotic ones of her own.

She glances down at my erection as I pull out a tissue to clean up after her release. I save my fingers for last.

The moment it looks like she's going to attend to me, I tell her to wait. "When we stop, I want my cock buried inside of you." Surprise lights her eyes. With her lips still parted, I run my thumb along her bottom lip. "As good as your mouth is, I think I'd rather bring you to the edge again."

And that's exactly what I do. I fuck her hard enough to rock the car in the dock's parking lot after asking Noah to take a walk so we could have a moment. I have her bite down on the leather to keep her as quiet as she can be.

It's much darker with the short hour it's taken to get to the dock, and cooler by the Hudson River. As I open the car door for Suzette, silently thanking Noah for parking in a rather private area of the lot, the breeze sweeps by us.

"I don't think I've ever taken a tour of New York at night on a cruise ship," Suzette comments softly as she steps out, her hand in mine. Her heels click on the pavement and she looks out toward the harbor.

I can barely focus on what she's said as the chill hits us. "Do you have a jacket?"

"I wasn't expecting to come out tonight."

"I'll have Noah deliver one." The moment I've shut the

door, I slip off my jacket that's far too large for her and wrap it around her shoulders.

"You don't have to," she says as she shakes her head, her locks falling down her shoulders as she does. She smiles up at me with a sweet, sated look on her face. "But I appreciate it."

With my arm wrapped around her back, I hum in response and search the dock for Trent's ship.

From where we're standing, I'm not sure which ship is his and where we should start.

"And they say chivalry is dead," she teases.

Without thinking much of it, I murmur, "If I'm going to fuck you in the back of my car, I can at least make sure you're comfortable after."

"And to think I just called you a gentleman."

"Mr. Bradford," Noah says behind me, clearing his throat.

If I could experience shame, I'm certain I'd feel it at this moment. "Noah," I say and turn to face him, not missing the glee that shines in her devilish eyes. "I was just about to message you.

"If you could see to it, Ms. Parks doesn't have a jacket this evening. Very much my fault."

"Say no more, sir."

"Thank you."

"Thank you so much," Suzette speaks up, "but truly—"

"Truly you will be cold once we set off, and as much as I adore you in my jacket, I'm not sure it's the look you'll be going for."

There's a pause where Suzette stares back at me, and I wonder if my little vixen is going to fight me on something so simple.

"Mr. Weston is near the northern end, I believe," Noah speaks before she can object. "His wife Laura is hard to miss tonight. And I'll see to it that there's a jacket on your shoulders that's more suitable, Ms. Parks." With a nod, he's off before Suzette can object. I make a mental note to give Noah a bonus for his discretion.

"You don't have to buy me things."

"It's a jacket," I state as if it's nothing.

"Come, the Brooklyn Bridge and the Manhattan skyline are waiting for us."

"It's why I love the city," she says and there's an awe in her tone that draws me closer. With my hand on the small of her back, she leans in closer. I fucking love it. Those walls of hers are crumbling down.

"The skyline?"

"How bright it is at night. How beautiful and lively."

"It is the city that never sleeps." Walking toward the railing, we take a moment to appreciate the towering steel lit with shades of blue and yellow lights. "It's gorgeous, isn't it?"

"Mm-hmm," I hum in agreement, watching her take in the view as the water crashes beneath us.

"I've never taken a tour of the city via cruise either. If you weren't here, I wouldn't."

Peeking up at me, Suzette questions, "You wouldn't have come?"

"I would have, and I would have made the deal before the ship left. It's the same with the galas and charity balls and all of these ... social gatherings. I stay at the bar, I meet and greet who I must and then I leave."

"All work and no play," she comments, her eyes locked on mine. There's a softness tonight I only got glimpses of before.

"Would you like to wait here for your jacket, or meet the hosts for the evening?"

"I think we should get on with it," she answers, shedding my jacket from her shoulders.

"That's not going to happen." I scold her lightly, slipping the jacket into place. "I wouldn't be caught dead wearing a jacket while you shiver."

"I won't shiver." The wind rushes by in that moment, as if to prove she's a liar.

A rough chuckle leaves me and I give her the option again. "We can wait here if you'd like or if you don't mind wearing my jacket for a moment, we can start the night."

"I think I don't mind either way," she says softly, staring up at me like she was before, although her gaze is ripped away the moment I hear my name in the distance.

"There you are!" Trent calls out.

"Well," Suzette whispers, "I suppose your jacket will do for now."

CHAPTER 8

SUZETTE

The boat cuts through the river below us as the skyline rises above. The bright lights twinkle against the black sky. Up close, it's intimidating but there's still something elegant about those tall buildings.

The air at the bow of the boat is crisp and clean. With both of my hands holding the railing, I breathe in deep, grateful for a moment alone after the last hour of socializing. My cheeks hurt from the constant smiling. I laugh when it's appropriate and keep everything light. This isn't my first time at a gathering that's … out of my league.

I'm sure it's obvious that I don't quite fit in, but it's gone well as far as I can tell. Champagne flutes clinked as we worked through the crowd, and the small gathering of women mostly gossiped about social circles I'm not privy to.

Most notably, the view is stunning.

I grew up in New York, but not in the city. I knew the dream of it, breathed in the hope of what NYC offers. I believe in this city. It will never cease to amaze me.

New York City is freeing in the same way my divorce was liberating.

Admittedly, that freedom came from the fact that I had security in my job. I could make it on my own and live the dream I've had since I was a little girl without fear. That was then. My hands twist against the cold, smooth metal. This is now.

Apprehension spreads through my gut. I can't deny the fear that my job might be on the line now. I've slept with Adrian and he's sending emails about gathering client lists like he wants to rearrange everything at the office. Or rather his "team" is. If I don't have that security anymore, then everything is at risk.

"You've been out here a while." The deep rumble from behind me is startling.

Adrian appears at my side by the railing, looking out with me. "I was spending time with my thoughts." Smiling at him, I step a bit closer. "Is your meeting done?"

"Yes."

"Did you seal the deal?" I ask him as he breathes in deep, looking over my shoulder to gaze at the skyline. He peers down at me, a charming smile at his lips. "Always, my little vixen."

With the heat in his eyes, I let out a nervous huff of a laugh and pull away.

"Dinner's about to start. Let me get you a drink."

It gives me a bit of relief that he's not pressing me about what's on my mind. I'm not sure how to talk about it with him yet. Adrian leads me back inside the cabin, the mood seeming a little more somber as more thoughts race through my mind. Thoughts of anxiety and anticipation about what's going to happen at work.

Adrian takes me by the elbow to guide me through the tables, stopping at the bar for a glass of wine. The ship is massive and spacious. It's obvious they spared no expense for this evening's outing. The group of women I was chatting with earlier are seated with their companions, dining on caviar as they overlook the river.

All the tables have been set with linen tablecloths and beautiful dishes. This is how the other half lives. It's elegance and convenience that will only ever be a dream for most.

"We're toward the stern ... for more privacy."

We reach our table, nestled in a corner with lit candles and the perfect view of the ship splitting the water that reflects the bright lights of the city. I stop at the edge, bracing myself, suddenly uncomfortable. With a firm hand he tilts up my chin. "What's wrong?"

"Just worried." The knot in my stomach ties tighter.

"About what?"

It takes great effort to keep my expression neutral, in case anyone may see when I say, "My job."

Light dances in his eyes. "It's after six."

"Unlike you, I can't just turn it off. I can't stop worrying about my responsibilities and wondering what's going to happen to my income … and what might happen between us."

There's a pause, a tension that gathers between us before Adrian pulls out my chair and tells me, "We can discuss it later, but I'm telling you, I don't want you to worry."

"As if I can just stop."

"You can. And you will."

"It's just hard to believe right now."

"Let me help you with that." His gentle smile is as confident as his touch. "You need to eat. Sit." He takes my wineglass from my hand, only a few sips gone, and helps me to my seat.

It's a bit chillier now than it was earlier and even with the beautiful double collar Mackage jacket Noah was gracious enough to have rush delivered before the boat set sail, it's brisk.

"May I?" Adrian asks, still standing as I take my seat. He moves the remaining chair around the table, dragging it to sit beside me.

"You'd rather sit next to me?"

"I'd rather have my arm around you."

There's comfort that's unexpected, in the way he simply wants to be with me. Next to me, with me, touching me. I crave it without realizing it.

The waiter comes by with appetizers: oysters on ice, bruschetta, and marinated olives with feta. Where we're seated, the chatter is muted and drowned out by the water, the breeze is comforting and it feels like the city has stayed awake just for us.

We're finished with our appetizers when Adrian orders two glasses of ice water.

"I'm all right with the wine," I tell him.

"I thought we could play a game," is his reply. "To keep your mind off work."

"What kind of game?" My cheeks are instantly flushed and hot, though no one seems to be paying attention to us, tucked away back here. "Would it be ... discreet?"

"Very," he says and his gorgeous pale blue eyes rest on mine as he smirks, "as long as you can keep quiet."

"I have no problem with that." The suggestive game is enticing, and there's no doubt I would much rather get lost in this man's touch than ruminate on matters I cannot control.

Just as I rest my hand on Adrian's thigh, the waiter returns and a hot blush creeps to my cheeks realizing I'm the one caught. The waiter only offers a polite smile, not saying a word as he sets down the goblets of ice water and then uncovers dinner: filet mignon and lobster tail with mashed potatoes and asparagus, all neatly arranged in a tasteful way.

My mouth waters instantly.

Adrian's quiet and commanding as he tells me, "Pick up your fork and make sure you appear to be eating, no matter what I do."

"Appear to be eating or actually eat?" My fork hovers over the plate.

"You should eat," he decides. "I'll try to be fair and give you time to chew and swallow."

Adrian looks down at his own plate and says, "Enjoy dinner. That's all you need to do."

Small talk ensues. About the city, the ever-changing neighborhoods and real estate. Nothing heavy, yet it chips away at who each of us is and what we want.

"Why am I not surprised that you live in Tribeca," I comment offhandedly knowing how damn expensive it is. Yet another checkbox on tonight's elite list that I could never fulfill.

That's when I feel his hand on my thigh underneath the table, pushing my dress up. My fork scrapes against the porcelain, giving away my surprise until I can steady myself. His touch goes up and up until his knuckles brush against my clit through my panties.

Cold shocks me so suddenly, I gasp.

"With a sound like that escaping those lips of yours," Adrian scolds, his tone teasing, "people will wonder if something happened to you."

He doesn't let up with the pressure against my clit and I struggle to perfect my expression.

"Keep your thighs apart," he murmurs. "That's the only way to play this game."

Circular motions of his knuckles make me hotter, increasing the heat until all at once he removes his hand.

My initial reaction is to object, but that's quickly silenced as he plucks a piece of ice from his glass and, with his eyes on mine, his hand disappears under the table. My lips part with a hiss as the cold hits my inner thigh first. He doesn't stop, slowly trailing it up.

I let out a breathy laugh. "That's freezing," I admit. "It's so, so cold."

"Sensitizing, isn't it?" he says quietly and casually spears a stalk of asparagus with one hand, while his other slips the ice up and down my slit until slowly he presses it inside of me. Goosebumps dance along my skin as I focus on my breathing and simply staying still.

Adrian repeats this process, bringing me to the edge and then stopping me with the freeze of an ice cube. Abruptly, he stops.

"You're going to give us away," he warns lowly, his lips at the shell of my ear and his warm breath tickling my neck.

That's when I realize my fork is fisted in my hand and my eyes were closed tight.

"I know you can do it. My little slut knows how to hide it. Don't you?"

My breathing is rushed when another piece of ice slips

along my skin, and my hand trembles. Adrian watches this with curiosity burning in his eyes.

"Oh my," I whisper and breathe, my eyes half-lidded.

"I want you to come for me."

"I don't think—" With two fingers he enters me, his fingers deft and knowing. As if he's memorized just how to get me off.

"I know you can. If you must, lay your head down on the table." The moment he suggests it, I obey, pushing the plate away and resting my head down.

He doesn't let up, not even when the waiter questions if I'm all right and he orders Dramamine for me.

The second his footsteps disappear, Adrian's touch becomes merciless and he whispers at my ear, "If you don't come for me right now, I swear to God I'll throw you over this table and fuck you until all of Manhattan hears you crying out my name. I couldn't care less about this deal if I can't even get my little whore to come on my hand."

My lips part, my warm breath heating my face still resting against the table and hidden by my arms. That's what does it. It's what brings me to the edge. I clench around him thinking of what he's just described.

The moment I'm granted my release, he removes his hand and it's only a moment after that his hand rests on my shoulder while rubbing soothing circles. Adrian informs the waiter that I will be fine.

"Take these, sweetheart," he says clear as day, without a trace of anything that's just happened in his voice.

"If she needs anything at all, let us know," the waiter says and I don't dare lift my head just yet. I'm flushed and shamelessly sated.

It's only once he's gone that I dare to peek up.

"Bad girl," Adrian admonishes me. "You'll do better for me next time, won't you?" he teases and I only blush harder.

Setting two small pills down on the napkin, he brings my plate back, placing it in front of me.

"The appetizers were ... delicious," he comments.

"You're shameless," I counter, still breathless and gather my fork once again.

"I'm hard is what I am," he tells me, cutting into his steak.

"Do you want me—"

"No. No, not here." He considers me for a moment. "I want to make sure you know what you do to me. Watching you come undone for me ... that's all I wanted."

I don't know what to make of him. He's ruthless. Confident. On the side of being arrogant. But the things he does to me make me forget everyone and everything else.

"You look like you want to say something," he comments, taking another bite. His food is quickly disappearing and mine's barely been touched.

"I thought you would be different."

"My reputation is not kind. I'm aware."

"They say you're an asshole and I thought it would be easy to hate you." It's the truth. And it slips out without censorship. Adrian smirks. "I've heard you're merciless."

"I am."

I guide my fork over my plate and lift a bite to my mouth. "Are you an asshole or are you merciless?"

"Both. I can be vicious." Adrian says this with a casual tone that makes me think he's telling the truth. Of course, I already know this about him. There's a reason the entire office is in a furor with him simply being in the building.

"I don't know what to make of you."

His eyes meet mine and his gaze lingers as if he's waiting for me to elaborate. My heart pounds with curiosity and fear that this will go badly and I won't have an office to go back to.

"There are people who earn big paychecks and then there are the people who write them," Adrian begins. "I wasn't born into wealth, but I watched my father work his way up to being one of those people who earned his paycheck. And then it was taken away from him after one wrong deal."

My body goes as cold as the ice he used to play with me earlier.

"I've looked into it since then," continues Adrian, "and it was a bad deal. He made a mistake. But that was after years of making the right decisions over and over, after working his way up only to be knocked down the second something went wrong. Not because it was deserved, but because he made too much and it would be too easy to give his tasks to someone else. Then the person who wrote the big check could simply make back that money by letting him go."

This is by far the most Adrian has ever shared with me, and my curiosity is piqued again. I don't know anything about his father, only what I've read about him, which is simple. He buys companies, breaks them apart, moves some departments around and eliminates others. He's the man writing the checks and doing the firing now.

"That company went under within two years," Adrian says quietly. Judging from his tone, this is important to him. The measured cadence of his words and the look in his eyes as he speaks.

"Without your father?" I manage to ask.

"Partially because of that. Partially because I bought the competitor. I hired my father. As the stock grew, I invested in other companies, including two crucial to my father's former employer … And I dismantled them."

Adrian uses a cool, almost bored tone to tell me this, and I'm even more afraid for my job now. He could do anything he wanted with the company. "Vindictive much?" I say, to cover the nervous pulse in my throat.

"He treated certain things, certain people, as if they were disposable. I showed him exactly what that meant. There are highs and lows in this business. Harsh decisions must be made. But the reasoning behind it is what matters. Is it for efficiency? For the bottom line? For power plays?"

"Why do you do it?"

Adrian's eyes flash. "Because if there isn't passion behind it, it shouldn't exist. It's a waste of time for everyone involved. It will fail, and the only ones who will benefit are the ones who are willing to sacrifice the purpose of it all." His deep voice is filled with conviction. Adrian believes what he's saying, and I imagine it's why he fired so many of the executives today and sent them all packing. He has a passion for this business, not simply an investment.

"I learned a hard lesson early on: if you can't beat them with morals and ethics, cut their throats and say that it's business."

A chill flows over my skin and numerous questions rest on the tip of my tongue. "I didn't buy Holt and Hanover to cut anyone's throat," he states before I can ask. "The numbers are still being run with slight changes." His tone is one of comfort, but the conversation is anything but. "When I know anything, you will as well. Do not worry."

I can only nod as a shiver runs down my shoulders and I realize we're back at the dock. The water is quieter and the chatter from the others much louder.

The waiter returns to check on me just then and he's relieved to hear I'm feeling better. If my head wasn't clouded with current topics, I would have blushed violently.

"Are you finished?" Adrian asks after time passes with easy silence, with a patient tone that says I could sit here for another hour, if I wanted.

Once again, I tell him the truth. "Yes." I put my napkin on the table next to my plate.

"Good. When we get to the car I want you on your knees," he mutters beneath his breath, standing up at the same time I do. A shiver returns, but this one is heated and causes flutters in places I shouldn't be concerned with in public.

"So demanding."

Adrian's smile seems to light up the dining area. "Are you just now learning that, Ms. Parks?"

CHAPTER 9

ADRIAN

The city blurs by, a streak of grays with splashes of colors as Noah speeds up down the avenue. It's late, far too late given I have an early morning meeting with the executives of a company based overseas. There's no doubt in my mind that rescheduling it would not go over well.

Leaning forward, I spread my knees, resting my elbows there and stretch my back, feeling the pull of it in my spine. Without thinking, I stare at the empty seat beside me, where Suzette was yesterday. The corners of my lips pull up, remembering how she squirmed, how easily she gave in. How she melts for me. And how much she loved it.

Today was hell. Meeting after meeting and when she

texted that she had plans tonight, I can't deny I felt loss. With her, I want every moment I can get. This evening held precisely none of them.

"Mr. Bradford?" Noah calls back, peering at me in the rearview although he doesn't use the intercom.

"Yes?" I answer him and then lean back in the seat, resting my head and meeting his gaze in the mirror.

"Shall I make it a habit of keeping the divider up between us when Ms. Parks joins you?"

The hum of the night surrounds us as I consider his question. There's no judgment; it's honest professionalism.

Something I've lacked today.

"I think it would serve us all well if you did, and I apologize if anything made you uncomfortable recently."

"Nothing at all, sir, just thinking of your lady."

Your lady. My brow rises, but my phone buzzes in my hand, interrupting my thoughts. There are only a few numbers I allow this late at night.

My father: *Did Wyatt send you the contract?*

My eyes roll back in my head as I inhale long and steady. My father is friends with his, and that's how we became acquainted nearly a decade ago.

My phone buzzes again: *Dale's here and we were wondering.*

Dale is Wyatt's father, rather protective but a supportive man.

I text him back quickly: *The lawyers have it atm.*

It occurs to me then that Suzette has yet to message. I'm

quick to type a message but then I delete it. I try another that's less ... domineering.

I prefer for that role to be played in person. Just as I finish typing her a message asking if she's home, a message comes through from my father, followed by one from her.

Suzette: *Just laying down for bed and thinking of you. Thank you again for last night.*

I ignore my father for a moment, choosing to message her: *The pleasure was all mine.*

She doesn't waste time replying: *You lie, Mr. Bradford. I enjoyed it immensely.*

With a satisfied hum, I sit back and see my father's messaged twice.

The lawyers will be fine with it.

Are you working this late? Please tell me you've cut back.

He's been on me for years now to work less. With the team in place and fewer projects, although they're costlier and more rides on their success, I've been able to slow down, little by little. Small steps toward a more "sustainable lifestyle," as my father refers to it.

Just got back from a date actually. I text him the white lie. It's not exactly truthful, but it will make him smile.

"Is that her?" Noah questions from the front. Again not using the intercom, and it takes me a moment to understand he means Suzette.

"Ms. Parks?"

"You have a smile for her. I can tell it's her. I have one that was just for my wife."

"Oh, calm down with that talk now, Noah," I joke with him. "We've only just met—"

"I told you Ann and I ... it was two weeks and then forever." His voice holds a hint of reverie.

"Yes, I know the story well." Noah's worked for me for the better part of a decade now. As my driver and at times my assistant when needed. "One day ... one day I'll have that," I say and then run my hand through my hair, thinking that *one day* seems to get farther and farther away as the years go by. "Ms. Parks is ... we are only getting to know each other."

"Is that what you kids call it nowadays?"

Letting out a brutish laugh, I turn my attention back to my phone.

There are emails and calendar notifications. My father messaged me about details of some buildings Wyatt is hoping to acquire, but he needs the capital first. My capital. As well as some questions about my date and whether it's serious.

Another message comes through, this time my mother, wanting to know about the date.

I debate on answering them, but I let my phone sit in my lap, thinking of Suzette at the dock yesterday and how easy it was. I haven't had that before. No one has ever fit so well, even if she fights me along the way.

As if she knows I'm thinking of her, a message comes

through: *I need to sleep.*

Then you should sleep, my little minx.

I watch the phone with anticipation, knowing she's typing something, but then deletes it. A moment passes and she starts again. My phone buzzes, with the messenger open: *I like being your little minx, I think.*

I like it too.

The moment I send my response, it doesn't feel good enough. It doesn't carry the weight of just how much I enjoy her simply being there. I follow up with:

When you sleep, I want you to dream of me.

Yes, sir.

CHAPTER 10

SUZETTE

Adrian fills my mind every hour that I'm awake, and most of the ones where I'm sleeping. His text messages make my pulse quicken with excitement.

I can hear how he would speak the words when I read them. It feels like falling. In only a week's time, I feel like I'm falling for him.

No one else at the office is fawning over him.

I'm often worked up and overheated, carefully avoiding him and the topic of him because everyone calls him the devil.

They complain about not knowing what's going to happen and how they think every task is in preparation for someone else to take over. Then there's me. I can't stop thinking of how he put that ice between my legs, and the soft groans that he makes when he fucks me on his desk. Purposefully avoiding the obvious and doing everything I can not to worry. Because he told me not to, even though all signs point to the company being sold off.

It's all ridiculous and overwhelming. If I wasn't fucking him, I might have quit already ... well, not if I couldn't take the clients with me. Maybe. I don't know. Like I said, it's all too overwhelming, so I choose to believe him. I'm doing everything I can to listen and not worry.

With my fingers tapping aimlessly on the keys, I have to snap myself out of it. Not that it matters; we're on a freeze with clients this week. I could lose my shit and it wouldn't make a difference in productivity. The only work that's getting done is paperwork and severance packages. I could be a nervous wreck like the rest of the office, or I can fantasize about the clock turning six.

Every day, I rock back and forth between the two of them.

A light knock at my door takes me out of my thoughts. A young brunette in joggers and a flowy tank stands in my doorway.

"Maddie," I say, greeting my friend for lunch. "I was wondering when you were going to get here." My chair rolls to the left as I push my keyboard to the side to make room for takeout.

Passing me a brown paper bag she sighs and says, "Sorry. Traffic was hell."

She's gorgeous, as she always is, but there's a sad curve to her mouth. "You okay?"

She takes the seat across the desk from me and opens her bag in her lap, waving me off with the other hand. "I think I need a man or a really good vibrator."

"I vote vibrator," I joke with a short laugh, unrolling the top of the bag without taking my eyes off Maddie. She's young, naive, and a romantic. A.k.a. the prime suspect for assholes. She barely cracks a smile. "Is that dipshit Daniel still on your mind?"

Maddie groans. "He's always on my mind, and I can't get him off of it. It's not fair. Why did such a shitty person have to get so far into my head?"

"That's how it always seems to be. The worse the person is for you, the more you think about them."

"Let's go out and go man shopping tonight. There's a new club down on Madison Avenue. It's like my grandmom always said, get over one by getting under another." She takes a bite out of her turkey club and guilt washes over me.

I haven't told Maddie about Adrian yet, and it seems like a betrayal of our friendship, almost. Suddenly I have no appetite. The chicken caesar wrap stays at the bottom of the bag.

I'm not sure what I would tell her. Being discreet means not blabbing your business to anyone who'd listen. I wince at the thought. Maddie's not just a random person. She's my friend, one of very few, and she's been my friend for far longer than I've known Adrian.

"I've looked up Lucifer," I joke. "He's hot as hell."

"Why don't you cuddle up to him?" Maddie half teases although her tone is dull. Her large doe eyes twinkle as she grins, pausing between bites to say, "Get a little action. Save the day. You'd be the office hero."

"The office needs a hero," I comment, keeping my tone light. "Everyone's nervous about their jobs now that entire divisions have been laid off."

My department has kept the same workload, but four people have been taken for interviews. Not by Adrian himself, but by some team he hired.

"Speaking of heroes," Maddie says, and then she talks about the new TV show she's been watching on HBO for the rest of the time we're eating. I'm grateful for the change in subject and somehow I've gotten out of going to the club with her this weekend. It's pleasant conversation and a much-needed break in the day. The wrap was decent too although I barely tasted it.

All I could think is that I should tell her. Maddie would keep my secrets and maybe she would smack some sense into me.

I know part of the reason I don't is because of that very fact: She would give her opinion, and what if it's to stop seeing him? What if she says it's wrong and it's going to end in failure and heartbreak? She's the romantic of the group, and yet I don't even have faith she would approve.

When she's gone, there's a small fire under my ass. A need to prove there's nothing at all wrong with it. We work during the day, play at night. I haven't changed who I am and there's nothing wrong with it.

This feeling that everything's up in the air isn't good for my productivity or anyone else's, and the only way to know what's going to happen is to ask him directly. And it's not six yet, so business is business.

Every single time I gather the courage to demand answers or terms, to know what the hell is going on so I have something I can tell everyone who needs answers, there are people in his office.

Adrian's secretary furrows her brow whenever I pass close to her desk. On my third trip, I decide to ask her what she knows. I imagine she's got to know something, given how close she works to Adrian. And any little piece of info I can bring back would be a win. "Hi there," I say, greeting her with a smile. Laying on the charm. "I'm Suzette. You're new to the company." My hip rests against her desk.

"That's right," she says with a tight smile. "Not new to Mr. Bradford, though. I'm Andrea."

There's a tinge that runs through me. It's a feeling I don't like. My gaze slips to this woman's hand, a woman who could be my mother, and I find a wedding ring back there. Jealousy is unbecoming and I can't believe I felt it for a second. In her white flowy blouse and pencil skirt, Andrea most certainly takes care of herself.

"How long have you been his secretary?"

"Oh, years and years. You know how it is with a good job. You stick with it."

"I do know about that." My stomach turns over. That's exactly why I'm here—to talk to Adrian about the future. This job saved me after my divorce and made it possible to have the freedom I gained, but if I'm let go, I'll be in an even worse position. "Sticking with it is usually for the best. I've heard he can be ..." I deliberately let my voice trail, waiting for Andrea to pick up where I left off.

She gives me nothing, tilting her head with her perfectly plucked brow raised and her hands folded in her lap. Touché. I finish it myself. "A bit ... ruthless."

"I would agree with that at times."

She nods and I do as well ... neither of us giving the other anything.

"If you've worked for him for that many years, you must have seen him take over a number of companies like this."

Her eyes widen. "Oh, yes. It can be unsettling for the people who have been there the longest. Adrian insists on changing things where they need to be changed instead of sticking with the status quo. It means a lot of shuffling around at the beginning."

I wince. "That's what I've heard ... the shuffling, though, that's—"

"Ruthless." Now she finishes it.

Hearing about a powerful man like Adrian shuffling people around doesn't soothe me when it comes to my own job. He's merciless when we have sex, and he must be the same way when it comes to business. He won't keep me on if it's not the right thing for the company. My throat tightens at the thought of being let go by him. Stomach turning, I breathe deeply to keep myself in check. I've had to do this many times over the years, working with men who didn't know how to listen to a woman.

Oddly, the thought of being fired from my job isn't the only thing at the forefront of my mind. Adrian is there as well. If I'm let go from this position, there will be no more meeting up at six for discreet activities. So his secretary's words aren't very reassuring. I hadn't considered how I might lose my job and Adrian at the same time. Though it's a bit presumptuous to think there's such a thing as losing Adrian when what we have is a fuck-buddy agreement.

"You work till six," she comments and now it's my turn for my expression to pinch.

"I do."

"I only noticed because of the submissions."

I pause, nodding but not contributing; it's her turn to show her cards.

"Mr. Bradford seems to have changed his habits," she says and leans back in her chair. "He never used to stay late. Once it was five o'clock, he went home. But it seems his preference, for this company only, is now six."

"Oh?" The back of my neck tingles.

"Mm-hmm," she hums.

"Well, that's something." Does she know? It's all I can think as she stares up at me. She's older, wiser maybe. I don't know. But everything in me is screaming that she knows.

"I'm sure he won't let you go," the secretary says, her expression innocent. "Seems to me you've been doing quite a bit for this company."

"I've done a lot of work," is my distracted reply. She might not let me in to see him, but that doesn't mean I'm any less hungry for information. I'm not sure how to phrase it, though.

"Can I tell you something?" she asks.

"Of course," I reply and my nervous voice betrays me.

"He seems to be distracted lately."

"Oh? I'm sure I wouldn't know anything about that."

She takes in my red cheeks. "Hmm. I think you might. I'm good friends with his driver."

I blush deeper. "I see."

Reaching for her glasses, she barely contains her cat-ate-the-canary grin. "If it were up to me, I'd let you in there, love, but I can't."

"Oh, I'm not—I don't do this kind of thing." A numbness creeps through me. How long have I worked here, only to potentially have my reputation ruined by the rumor mill? I have no idea if I can trust this woman in the least, although she seems friendly. I did just lie to her face, though.

Restlessly, I shift my weight from one foot to the next. I stop as soon as the secretary notices. "I really don't do this," I say again.

"Neither does he," she says, leaning in, her tone friendly still. It eases something in me. "I mean it. I've worked with him for over a decade now. Mr. Bradford ... he doesn't behave like this. He's strict with his regimen and occasionally a woman has come in to speak with him. But it's never ... like this."

CHAPTER 11

ADRIAN

"You know how I know you want to push me today and not in a good way?" I question the vixen at my side. Her cherry-red heels clip on the pavement as I open the door, waving toward Noah that I've got it. The spring day is a cloudy one, with gray skies and the threat of rain clouds.

"How's that?" she asks, gripping the door frame, one shoe inside the car, the other firmly planted on the curb. She stares at me from over her shoulders, the wool coat perfectly hugging her frame.

"Because you're eager to get me alone in this car. I didn't have to fight you."

Her smile is wicked, her rose petal lips trying all they can to stay pursed, but they fail. "Inside," I command her and she obeys, properly and politely as I shut her door for her, knowing damn well she's going to try to get information out of me. While I sat through meeting after meeting, she came looking for me. Andrea let me know. She suggested I order flowers, of all things.

I'm not sure what exactly she thought Suzette was coming to see me for, but if I had to guess, with the cars buzzing by us and the nightlife of the city turning vibrant, it's about her department and the upcoming meetings.

With a steadying inhale, I climb into the back seat and shut the door.

"I tried to speak to you all day." She doesn't waste a second. She peeled her coat off, laying it across her lap and at first glance, I'm given a damn good look of her breasts. Whatever contraption she's wearing has pushed them to the top of her blouse which hangs low, I presume to display cleavage.

Not fair.

Reaching for my seat belt, I prepare myself.

"I had roundtables with my team." The belt clicks into place and the tick of the blinker is barely heard as Noah rolls up the partition, allowing us privacy.

"Your team who's talking to *my* team," Suzette stresses and I can't help but to let out a chuckle.

Leaning my head back, I turn to face her.

"I don't find it funny," she tells me and there's a hint of

hurt there.

"Because you aren't in control," I tell her honestly.

With her hands in her lap, she fidgets with her fingers and tells me, "I just need to know what your plans are."

"It's after six, Suzette." I'm soft with the reminder.

"I don't like this." She's equally soft with her disappointment. It's unsettling. Not anger; she's genuinely upset.

"It's okay to be uncomfortable. That's how progress is made," I tell her, in an attempt to ease her mind.

"I suppose I could leave you uncomfortable then?" It's not quite a tease or a threat, but some combination of the two.

My response is firm. "Don't tempt me to punish that mouth of yours before we've had dinner." She swallows, the threat coming through as it should. To remind her that she loves what I do to her, that right now the office is behind us and we're to get lost in each other.

Her posture remains stiff, though, and her gaze guarded.

In an attempt at a truce, I rest my hand on hers, and she reciprocates by turning her small hand to hold mine. "Thank you," I murmur and then run my thumb along her soft skin.

"Please, answer me one thing," she presses and I close my eyes to respond with a short nod.

"What are you going to do with it?"

"With what?"

"The company?"

I remain silent. As if it were so simple to have a one-sentence answer, or to even know what would be best so early on.

"A split-up? Go public for shares? I looked into the other companies under your LLC, so I doubt you have a merger in mind."

When I finally open my eyes and look back at her, fear lingers in every nuance.

I debate on confiding in her, knowing how quick office rumors are to spread and the chaos that little bits of information can create. But then she utters a single word, staring back at me like I could make every little worry she has vanish. "Please."

"The plan is a split-up and the merger of the new entity and another company I have in mind ... if possible."

She doesn't hesitate to question, "And what about the other? The original entity? The departments that aren't useful for the merger?"

I'm silent, half wondering if she's playing me. If all of this was a setup and she's pumping me for information. "There are inefficiencies that cannot be overlooked."

"Where does my department—"

My tone is harsher than I'd like as I interrupt her. "Not everything has been decided." Gentling it, I add, "You don't need to worry."

"As your lover or as your employee?"

"When I tell you that you don't need to worry, I need you to believe it. I need you to trust me."

She's silent, and every second that passes feels as if another weight has been added to my chest. It's obvious I haven't eased her concerns in the least. She wants a definitive answer and I can't give her one. I can't say anything with certainty.

"No more. It's after six and I promise, I will make time for you at work. As your boss. Right now I only want to be your lover, as you put it."

It seems for a moment that she'll say something; her lips part and she inhales, but then her gaze falls and she merely nods. Not looking back at me.

"Thank you for respecting the boundary."

"I don't like it," she whispers, at first looking out the window but then she meets my gaze.

"You look gorgeous squirming, though." I pick up her hand and kiss the back of it, our fingers laced together. "It would please me if you wouldn't worry."

In a breath she laughs, as if it's the most ridiculous thing she's heard. "Is that all you need, for me to just not worry?"

Softly, I repeat the reassurance, "You will be all right."

She's quick to tell me, "It's not just me." She shakes her head. "I'm sorry. I'm done. I'm done for right now. I won't bring it up again."

"I want you to confide in me, I do. I wish I had the answers for you, but I don't."

"When you do, will you tell me?" There's hesitancy in her tone, but also hope.

"The second I know, I will tell you everything."

Her shoulders drop slightly and she sinks deeper into the seat, not responding other than a nod and a soft, "Thank you."

A moment passes, and the tension lessens.

"I had a hard day today," I confide in her, our fingers still intertwined.

"I did too," she speaks softly. "Fridays are long days, but at least we have the weekend." Just when I think that's all she'll say, she offers, "Can I do anything?"

"Do anything?"

"To make anything better."

"Not with work—"

"No, with you. Can I ..." she trails off and tosses her hand in the air, the one I was holding. "Can I yell at someone, or massage your shoulders? I could ..." she pauses and rolls her eyes. "I don't know, write an angry email or order us takeout for dinner." In my silence, her tone is laced with exasperation when she says, "I could ... I don't know. What would make it better?"

"You could kiss me."

"Would that make it better?" she questions, the hint of a smile on her lips.

"Yes. If you kissed me, it would."

She doesn't waste a moment, and when she kisses me, her hands wrapped around my face, I can feel her smile.

CHAPTER 12

SUZETTE

The New York skyline is much different from the windows of Adrian's penthouse. I'm used to feeling as if it's towering over me, but in his living room we're a part of it. In the heart of Tribeca surrounded by historic industrial buildings and new construction that's all steel and glass.

It's the epitome of New York.

It almost seems like a movie backdrop is wrapped around the entire room. Floor-to-ceiling windows that, with a touch of a button, darken for privacy surround us. Every other day, Adrian introduces me to more wealth than I've experienced in the years I've planted roots in this city.

Behind me, he busies himself in the foyer answering a

call. The design is open concept but so far away, I feel lost in the view. Even his furniture seems to play a part in the city.

It's the perfect layout for a home with so much luxury. Hardwood floors shine under my feet and the neutral color scheme is fresh and strong. He has high ceilings and windows that kiss those ceilings, and beneath is a living room with sumptuous leather furniture that looks like it cost a mint.

Nothing in his home is out of place. There's not a single ounce of clutter, which adds to the masculine energy. It even smells like wealth, if ever there was a scent, one so clean it makes me a little jealous. I can imagine the people it would take to make a home look like this. A housekeeper at least, and others to make sure the walls and furniture stay perfect. The view alone is worth millions.

I can hardly keep my mouth closed as he gives me the tour, passing quickly by his bedroom and ending up back in the living room. "I didn't realize just how wealthy you are." I swallow thickly, my fingers playing at the hems of my silk sleeves.

The last time I felt awe like this was when I was flying into New York City for the first time. I couldn't believe I was finally going to live here, in a place I'd dreamed about for so long.

Adrian grins, slipping his arm around my waist. "I'm certainly not the richest man in New York."

"How very modest of you," I teasingly respond although my normal bite is lost.

There's a deep rumble from his chest, a short hum. I've

noticed him do it a few times now and with it, his hand drops lower, to the side of my hip and his thumb rubs soothing circles there.

It causes a tension, a nervousness inside of me. It's more *serious*. Because I crave it. I want more of that masculine hum of satisfaction.

Being in his personal space and seeing his things and furniture is way beyond what I ever thought I'd do with him. I'm nervous to get it right and keep my cool, but I'm a strange mixture of giddy and hot. The more I learn about Adrian, the harder it will be when things end between us. I'm not sure I want things to end between us. Which only adds more to the feeling of not having the upper hand.

I certainly don't want them to end here, in his beautiful penthouse with all his fancy furniture and Adrian in his suit from the office. Despite working all day it's still crisp. I'd like for him to take it off, or to play the game we always play ... but in his home, we don't have to rush.

"Are you all right?" he asks, his voice low.

"I'm fine."

"Do you want a drink?"

I nod. A drink would be good. Something to hold in my hands and busy myself with.

"Let's step into the kitchen, then." In Adrian's kitchen, which is an elegant, masculine space with dark marble countertops and tall reclaimed wood shelves, he takes down two cut glass tumblers. Light bends through them, refracting as he cradles them in his large palms. Even his tumblers reek of wealth. "What would you like?" he asks.

"You choose," I offer, not knowing what's in his kitchen.

"Whiskey?" he questions. "I have a favorite you may not have tried before."

"I don't mind whiskey."

"Chocolate cream cold brew whiskey," he speaks clearly, opening cabinets and leaving me alone by the kitchen island, standing quite alone in the expansive space.

Once he has what he needs, the bottles lined up and large spherical ice cubes taking up space in the tumblers, he strips off his jacket so he's just in his shirt from the office. Like his suit, his dress shirt is still pristine after a day of sitting in meetings and restructuring the company. My mouth waters at the thought of what's hidden under the belt around his waist and the white shirt above.

How did we come to be here? How did I find myself in this penthouse, with a man like him?

"If you don't care for it, I'll happily drink both and get you something else," he offers and I nod a thanks, deciding I should take that seat at the island after all.

He's capable in the kitchen, mixing this drink like he's made it a thousand times before. I have another flash of jealousy. Maybe he has, for some other woman, though it's none of my business who he brings here or who he makes drinks for. It comes and goes, leaving me questioning how much he's gotten to me. We've both been with other partners. And this, whatever is between us, is mutual.

Evening light glows around him as he tells me, "Let me know what you think."

"Thank you," I tell him as he hands me the heavy glass. The first sip goes down smooth. "Wow." I never would have guessed chocolate and whiskey would be a combination so easy and delectable. He's made it better than any bartender could have. It overwhelms me, how good it is.

"You like?" he questions, standing and leaning against the island.

"I do."

"Now that you've seen mine, I'm wondering about yours," he says, sipping his whiskey.

"My place is nothing like this," I comment, a bit worried, but also blunt. I'm sure he's aware. I don't come from *this* kind of money and my position certainly doesn't pay a salary where I could afford anything close to this in my lifetime.

Adrian sips his own whiskey, which he takes straight.

"I imagine you bring work home?" he asks.

"I prefer to stay at the office, but yes. My apartment is small. When I split with my ex, I sold off everything and bought a place in the West Village that I'd wanted for so long."

"Hell's Kitchen is fitting for you." I nearly tell him I'm barely there anymore, although I still love the neighborhood, but then I realize what he's revealed and discussing my apartment location seems unimportant.

"How did you know where I live?" I question and then answer for myself. "Did you snoop in the company files?"

"Of course I did. When I saw you that first day staring at me across the conference table, I already had your number."

"Well, that's not fair," I say with a pout, although it comes out a lust-filled whisper.

"I don't play fair."

"So you liked me while I hated the thought of you?"

He nods. "It's easy to hate the devil. So no offense taken."

I laugh, the nervousness dissipating. The drink Adrian made for me is helping. His expression intensifies, though, and he takes another sip of whiskey. "If it makes you feel any better, I don't think you're the devil anymore." Without thinking much of it, I raise my drink and confide in him, "That name is solely reserved for my ex-husband now."

His next question is casual: "What happened between you and your ex?"

Immediately I regret bringing Carl up in conversation at all. His name is the equivalent to an ice water bath.

I'm over that man, and I'll never want him again, but it still causes an old pain in my heart to talk about it. Luckily, the pang of betrayal is over quickly, and I can answer Adrian honestly. "He cheated ... with the company secretary."

Anger darkens his features. "So he was a fucking idiot.

Got it."

"No. Not an idiot. He was a manipulative bastard and damn good at it." My throat is tight as I correct him, once again feeling like a fool. "It wasn't just once, either. He had an affair for over two years. He used her to get details he shouldn't have been privy to."

Adrian takes a step closer and puts a hand on my shoulder. "I'm sorry," he says, his voice rumbling through me. "I'm sorry he hurt you and took advantage of you." He seems to make a decision. "My last ex was somewhat similar when it came to dishonesty."

Setting the glass down I admit to him, "I googled your name and love interest."

"You tried to look up my dating history?" He grins at me as if it's comical. "Did you find anything?"

"No," I state and he chuckles at my pursed lips.

There's almost no information online about Adrian's love life, as if it's been purposefully kept offline or scrubbed from the internet. There are companies that will do that for a person, and Adrian has enough money to hire them. Though most people don't care so much about erasing their exes from history.

"What happened with your ex?"

He drains his glass and pours another, taking in a deep breath. Just then, the intercom at his door rings, stealing his attention.

"One moment," he tells me and Adrian goes to answer.

"Food's here, Mr. Bradford."

"Bring it up."

It's quiet as he pours his whiskey, and I attempt a bit of small talk thanking him for dinner.

A doorman appears a minute later, in gray slacks with a shiny black name tag on his crisp white shirt, and two bags in hand. I cling to the tumbler, feeling out of place once again.

Adrian takes the bags out to the living room, where there's a massive sofa and a coffee table large enough to dine on.

As I slip off the stool, he opens the bags and lays out the containers on the table.

"The view is better in here," he tells me and when I reach the sofa, my hand on the soft leather, he peeks up at me to add, "and touching you will be far easier here."

A blush creeps up into my cheeks and I take the seat next to him. The savory smells of basil and marinara waft toward me.

"Italian?"

"Have you had Scalini Fedeli before?"

I shake my head gently, glass still in hand. "I haven't."

There's that hum again, that satisfied hum coming just before he balls up the paper bags. Rising from his seat, he tells me I'm going to love it.

As he plates the food, capellini with prosecco, porcini ravioli and arugula and buffalo mozzarella salad, my mouth waters. I do however notice that the conversation from the kitchen has stopped altogether.

Maybe he's not going to tell me. It's obviously a painful subject if he's just going to move on from it. Curiosity flares again, but I don't want to ask the question. I'd rather sit with him, enjoy this meal and wait for more of those deep rumbles from him.

"She never loved me," Adrian says, breaking the silence after the food is plated. "She never even wanted to be with me. She was with someone else the entire time."

"Oh my God." My heart breaks for him. I know this feeling so well. I wish I didn't, because it means my ex was a horrible person who wasted my time, but I know the betrayal that's coursing through his veins. It makes you feel so sick and stupid. Like you should have known all along what was happening, but you didn't.

"He told her to sleep with me because he wanted her to persuade me into certain deals."

"That is ..." Horrible. Worse than horrible. Devastating. It would make it hard to continue trusting people in business after that. Almost impossible. No wonder Adrian rearranges companies to such an extent. He doesn't truly trust anyone to be what they say they are.

"We were together for nearly six months before I realized."

"I'm sorry." I set the tumbler into my lap, both hands cradled around it. His focus is on his plate. His fork twirls the pasta around but he doesn't eat.

His eyes find mine and he offers me a smile that doesn't

reach his eyes when he says, "Maybe it's not polite dinner conversation."

"It's fine. I want to know more about you."

He gestures at the food on the coffee table. "You must be hungry," he says, and I know this part of the conversation is over.

My appetite has vanished, though, apart from small bites, which are delicious. We eat in relative silence. I'm sick on his behalf, and on mine. I never thought Adrian Bradford and I would have something like this in common—such complete betrayal by an ex. I guess betrayal doesn't care if you're rich. It can find you anywhere.

"What do you think?" he questions.

"About what?"

He huffs a small laugh, taking another bite before glancing at my half-eaten plate.

"Oh, it's delicious. I—You were right. It's delicious."

He's barely touched his plate as well. "I'm not as hungry for dinner as I thought I'd be."

"Me either."

A moment passes as he leans back, the sofa groaning under his weight. The plates stay where they are on the table, the empty tumblers of whiskey next to them.

"I'll never do that to you," he murmurs, his gaze drifting to my lips.

I turn onto my side, lifting my knees up and letting my

heels fall to the floor so I can rest my legs on the edge of the sofa. "I won't either. Cheating and lying are—"

"For assholes who can live with their misery," he says, finishing the statement for me.

I rest my cheek on the back of the sofa, and my hand slips into his. "Yeah."

As if he senses my thoughts, he says, "I want to get lost in you."

I don't have a chance to respond, only to part my lips as he crashes against them.

As soon as he touches me it's like we're back in the office, frantic for each other. He strips off my clothes with brutal efficiency. A gasp leaves me as he lifts me, forcing my legs to wrap around his hips.

I think he might take the floor, but instead he takes me to the windows looking out over the city. He's still fully clothed, save for the top buttons undone from my efforts a moment ago.

My stomach drops at the height of the building but Adrian murmurs in my ear, "You're safe here, safe from everything except being my fuck toy. Isn't that what you said you wanted?"

I wonder if they can see me. There's no other building this tall, but it would only take someone craning their neck to see me bared to the powerful man behind me.

My answer is a moan. He puts both my hands on the cool glass. "Keep your hands up," he commands me. "And spread your legs." My breasts press against the glass as my hips are pulled against his crotch. His erection pushes against my ass.

His hand dips down between my thighs and teases up until he's stroking my clit, alternating it with pushing his fingers inside me until I whimper for more. Then he focuses relentlessly on my clit until I come on his fingers with a cry, shaking against the windowpane. My legs nearly give out and I cling to Adrian as best I can, holding on to him to keep my balance. His lips trail down my neck as he toys with me, bringing me closer and hotter to yet another release. It's hot and my pulse races, for the sheer force of my orgasm and from the view. The chill of the glass is at odds with how my body hums. He plays me like he knows every inch of me, and I fucking love it. I love what he does to me.

He tells me, "I think I'll fuck you here." His fingers slip lower, to a place I've only experimented with once. My eyes widen slowly and my lips part in an O. "Have you had anal before?"

I swallow thickly before answering, "Not in a long while."

"Did you enjoy it?" he questions and I rest my head back, staring down at the city. "It was ... different. We didn't get far," I admit. A college fling once tried ... we were drunk and lube was scarce. "It was a no go for lack of ... preparation."

A deep rumble of consideration comes from his chest as he seems to consider what I've told him. "Are you curious?" he asks.

"Yes," I admit, my heart racing.

"And you would you trust me to do my due diligence?" he questions and I can feel his smile against my neck. His fingers play at my clit again and my "yes" becomes a moan of approval. The thought instantly makes me nervous, but I would let Adrian do anything. I trust him.

"Lie down for me over here," he says, picking me up and taking me to his sofa. At first I yelp in surprise, clinging to him, but it quickly turns into a short laugh, smiling into the crook of his neck.

He's gentle as he sets me down on the soft leather cushion. "Wait here."

He comes back a moment later and puts me into position on his couch, on my belly, knees bent slightly. I'm quick to grab a pillow, laying my cheek against it and wondering what he'll feel like ... *there*.

Adrian kneels behind me and spreads me wide, his fingers playing at that place, cool and slick with lube. He pushes one finger inside, then two. It's an odd pressure and it makes me tense slightly before relaxing. The simple act heats my entire body and with it, my head thrashes and I moan gently into the pillow.

"How does it feel?" he questions.

"Good," I respond in a groan as his other hand finds my clit, his fingers still in my ass. "Fuck," I moan into the pillow.

"Tell me if anything feels uncomfortable," he tells me. "This shouldn't hurt, Suzette. It should feel good." All I can do is nod with my eyes closed. The sensation is all consuming, tingling every inch of me. With a whimper, I swear it's more sensitive and more illicit to be fucked like this.

He shifts us to the floor, which gives me a sensation of stability that the couch didn't, and I feel the head of him against me. I take in a quick breath.

"Push back," he orders, and I do. My body goes hot as he presses inside.

My hands fist the pillows and he tells me to relax.

"I want you to enjoy this," he whispers at the shell of my ear, his warm breath and gentle kisses adding to the overwhelming sensation.

With my eyes half-lidded, my lips part and I push back. Strangled moans pour from me. "That's my good girl," he urges me on, slowly pulling out and then pushing back in. Adrian murmurs things behind me but doesn't rush. It's very slow, and it makes me all the hotter. The full sensation turns to something else, something needy and undeniably pleasurable. Inch by inch I push myself back on him until he's fully inside me.

It's that last thrust that seems to shock my system. My eyes go wide and it feels too much, too hot, too full. Just too much.

"Oh," I gasp. Biting down on my lip, I utter a small grievance. "Stop, no. I don't know." It happened too fast, out of nowhere. He stops at once, stilling and my hand grabs the top of his.

"It's all right. How do you feel?" he questions. Fuck, it's

just so much. I want it, I want him. *I want this.* It's a sweet mix of pleasure and pain.

"Scared," I admit to him, remembering how much it hurt before. It was nothing like this. Not at all, but with a cold sweat on the back of my neck, I swallow down the unwanted memory.

"Just breathe," he says softly. "Give me a word that means stop."

"Whiskey," I say, the first thing that comes to mind.

"I'm going to move, Suzette."

He does, and it feels overwhelming to the point of paralyzing. There's not an ounce of control left for me; all I can do is hold on. I've never been taken in such a forbidden way before. Adrian is slow at first, then faster and deeper. I clutch a blanket he's thrown on the floor beneath us. With one hand on my clit, he takes full advantage of pushing me to the edge.

His thrusts get harder and deeper still and if it weren't for his lips on my neck that beg me to kiss him, I would be writhing beneath him.

"What's your word, Suzette?"

"Whiskey," I whisper, feeling the pleasure build and build.

"Good. I need you to remember that."

I almost ask him why, but he doesn't give me enough time. Adrian holds me down and fucks me ruthlessly. With deep strokes, he takes me like I'm his fuck toy.

I come instantly, his name on my lips and pleasure like I've never felt before rocking through me.

CHAPTER 13

ADRIAN

Exhaustion lays heavy against me, in the best of ways. The city lights creep through the edge of the curtain and cast a soft glow in the bedroom. The bed is warm and Suzette's body is molded to mine under the sheets. Her back to my front, my hand over hers. She makes this little humming sound every time I kiss her just beneath her ear. It's addictive. And when I sleep, I pray I hear it. The contentment, the satisfaction. I could see myself devoted to that soft sound.

"Did you enjoy it?" I question in a whisper at the shell of her ear.

Her response is a hum, a sated one cloaked in sated fatigue. My cock twitches at the memory.

"You'll tell me if it hurts," I whisper, bringing my hand to her hip as she presses her ass against me.

"Mm-hmm," she murmurs. She's quick to take my hand back, slipping her fingers through mine. Her eyes stay closed. She's well and thoroughly fucked, and after the night we've had, sleep should come easy.

All I can think is that I didn't ask to fall for her. It wasn't a part of any plan.

Every detail in the beginning was something I had planned. But she was unexpected, and *this* is entirely unexpected. Falling for her feels like it changes everything. I don't know what exactly changed, but everything feels different.

"I'll dream of you," she says.

"As you should," is what I reply. I bite my tongue before I let slip, *I'll dream of you too.*

If you're reading this, put your phone down and listen to your father.

My mother's text shows on the screen as I pick up my BlackBerry. I can't help but huff out a humorless laugh before setting it back down and tending to the pan on the stove.

The smell of bacon fills the kitchen as I flip the pancake one last time before slipping it off the skillet and onto the pile of six on the plate.

The fresh fruit was already sliced and prepared. All I had to do was pour the mix of cantaloupe, berries, and watermelon into the small bowl.

I'm not a chef by any means, but I can manage a simple breakfast.

The stack of pancakes joins the table next to the syrup and butter. Deeming it acceptable, I glance behind me toward the stairs deciding to wait until Suzette is up so she can join me. My BlackBerry buzzes again and I'm not certain if it's my father, telling me I need to take the weekend off, or my mother, agreeing with him. It could also be a work email, calendar notification or someone else who needs something from me.

With a black coffee in hand, I stalk to the adjacent living room and peer out of the windows overlooking the early morning in the city. It's already bustling beneath us.

This city never sleeps and, if you want to keep up with it, you can't either. The only thing that stops me from heading to my office is the knock on my door.

"Come in," I call out, knowing exactly who it is.

"Mr. Bradford," Noah greets me, carrying a variety of large department store bags in different colors, half of them with tissue paper peeking out. "This should do, I hope."

"Have you got everything?" I question, very much focused on the details beneath Suzette's clothing.

The older man nods, professional but with a knowing look as he sets the bags down. "Ann selected the delicates."

His sport coat and dark jeans are evidence that he has plans, more than likely with his wife.

"I appreciate it. Please let her know I am grateful."

"Is there anything else, sir?"

"Not at the moment."

"I'll be off then," he says and waves a short goodbye before glancing around the room, I imagine to spot the lady these clothes are intended for.

Much to my gratitude, the front door closes before Suzette quietly makes her way into the room. Her bare feet padding softly on the hardwood floor give her away. With her hair a messy halo, and dressed only in one of my undershirts, she could not possibly look more fuckable.

My grip on the mug in my hands tightens as I suppress a groan.

"Good morning," she offers, brushing her hair from her face. As her arms fold in front of her she gets reacquainted with my penthouse, glancing around before stopping in front of the set table.

"Good morning. Your clothes arrived." I motion toward the bags with the mug. "Coffee's on as well. Should I make you a cup?"

With surprise lightening her gaze, it dances between the bags and myself. "I'm sorry, did you say clothes arrived?"

"I think you could use some caffeine," I state rather than answering her. As I make my way to the kitchen, the tissue paper crinkles behind me.

"You ordered these for me?"

I pour her a cup, listening to the sounds of her opening each bag. "You needed something to wear home. Cream and sugar?"

"Please." Tentatively, I take in her posture. She's not unfamiliar with wealth, but I imagine it can be difficult for a woman like Suzette to readily accept.

"I should pay you back," she murmurs. I imagine she's attempting to tally the total.

"It's a gift."

"You didn't have to," she tells me, still holding an crimson silk shift dress with both of her hands.

"You keep saying that and I'll keep reminding you, it's because I want to." Setting her coffee on the table, I add, "Besides, I will very much enjoy seeing you in that dress." It's that deep red shade she seems to love so much. "I just hope it fits you."

"You're too much," she tells me, and I catch her gaze. "Thank you."

Good. That's all she needs to say.

"And breakfast?" She finally sets the dress back into the shopping bag, careful with the fabric, and gives me a simper. "You made breakfast?" She selects a small chunk of fruit.

"I thought you might have an appetite this morning.

"You would be right. I'm famished."

"I was thinking breakfast and then a shower?"

"As much as I like the smell of you and your body wash, I don't have anything to shower with."

"Everything you need should be in one of those." I motion toward the bags.

"Toiletries?" Again she seems surprised. Nodding, I take the seat across from her, making my plate of bacon and pancakes.

She seems shy as she speaks. "Thank you for letting me stay overnight ... and for all of this."

What kind of men has she been with? Did she think I'd fuck her and then send her home in a taxi?

Her apprehension fades as we eat.

"What are your plans for the day?"

"I'm behind on a contract for—" she starts, picking up a slice of bacon and then pauses. "What are the rules for the weekend?"

A short chuckle leaves me and I smirk at her. "We can negotiate those terms, Ms. Parks."

There it is. Her gorgeous smile and lightheartedness.

"I would like to spend the day with you, but I'm a bit behind with work." She sighs dreamily and adds, "A man has been distracting me."

I hum in agreement. "I know what you mean. There's an exceptionally beautiful and stubborn woman who's been distracting me as well."

Her simper widens and she rocks slightly in her seat.

"You look gorgeous, by the way." She blushes, as if she's a

shy little thing. Does she know how all of these facets of her have me more and more addicted?

I offer, "We could plan on working and fucking, fucking and working. Occasionally we must eat, though."

The smile dims as she lays her arms on the table, slightly more serious. "As much as that sounds exactly like the productive weekend I'd enjoy, I'm a little sore and I think I'd like to work from home."

I can't help that the corner of my lips tips up in an asymmetric smile. "Sore?"

She blushes again. "I think I may need to rest for the day, if you don't mind."

Before I can feel any kind of disappointment she questions, "What are your plans for tonight?"

"Wide open, Ms. Parks."

"Would you like to go on a date with me?"

"You're asking me out?"

"Officially. Yes. I think the weekends ... maybe we could date on the weekends?"

My smile matches hers. "I think I'd like that."

CHAPTER 14

SUZETTE

It's difficult, and unladylike, to eat yogurt and talk at the same time, but I'm managing it. Gail shovels a handful of almonds and raisins into her mouth as well, completely unfazed. We're both rushing through lunch and it's not uncommon in the least. Today is different, though. It feels as if everything is riding on this one task delegated from the "team."

Projected profits and client referrals based on previous numbers. A.k.a., how profitable is our division on its own? I'm more than certain we'll impress. Perhaps it's cocky or arrogant, but I know we're damn good at what we do and, as Gail so eloquently put it, it's time to whip our dicks out.

Lunch break be damned.

Maddie sits on one end of my desk, watching the conversation as she eats her caesar salad, and another of our coworkers is at her side. His name is Dale and Dale is ... well, he's Dale. He's got a sharp eye for marketing but his social skills are subpar. So he stays in his cubicle avoiding us as much as he can.

Today, I wish he'd done just that. There's an uneasiness about him and it puts a damper on the atmosphere that would otherwise be motivating.

"No, listen," I say to Dale. "I have an idea I want to pitch to you before we part ways again and you leave us to the figures."

"I'm not sure you should be pitching any ideas." He gives me a look that definitely means something and my face goes hot.

"What do you mean? I always pitch you ideas. It's no different for me to do it right now."

He arches an eyebrow. "Even with all the rumors flying around the office?" At once, my ears turn red hot. Gail pauses mid-chew, her dark brown eyes going wide and Maddie peeks up from her salad.

My heart drops in nervousness. "What rumors?"

"People have seen you with a certain someone," Dale says, his gaze darting toward the elevator.

"Who?" Maddie asks. *Fuck. Fuck, fuck, fuck.* With numb fingers I drop the mostly eaten yogurt to the small trash can.

As I do, I shoot her a look that gives her all the information she needs to know. Betrayal doesn't pair well with the sweet yogurt. It tastes far too sour.

Her mouth drops open. Two weeks of seeing Adrian nearly every day, and it was bound to happen. Shakily, I sip my water and take a few deep breaths to calm down, not responding at all to Dale.

"You're seeing him, aren't you?" Gail questions to my left. All eyes are on me and I fucking hate it. I knew this would happen. Office trysts *always* get out. I just wish it wasn't today of all freaking days.

Dale watches me carefully, as if he's not sure he can trust me anymore. I don't like that feeling. It's a sensation of being accused of something, though he is right that I'm seeing Adrian.

I nod in confirmation. The corners of Dale's mouth turn down. "So he sleeps with you on the weekend and then fires your coworkers on Monday."

A chill runs through me at his bluntness, but my back straightens.

Sighing, I put the bottle of water down on my desk. "That's pretty much how it is." My tone is bitchy yet stern as I meet his gaze head-on.

"And none of that has anything to do with the last decade of work I've put into this client list. So," I say and glance over my shoulder at Gail, "back to putting together this presentation because as much as I wish fucking Adrian would save our asses, we both made it very clear that lines would not blur." I pause, waiting for Dale to say anything at all. For

Maddie or Gail to pipe up.

A long moment passes with a heat tingling at the back of my neck.

"What if you tried blow jobs too?" Maddie says, then shrugs and Dale shakes his head although there's a hint of his smile showing.

Gail is less than impressed. "I need a moment," is all she says before walking out, leaving that pit in my stomach to weigh heavier.

That particular feeling only grows as the day progresses. Each time, it grows and grows until I feel like I could throw up.

The rumor is confirmed within minutes. It's easy to tell when each of them know.

Dale was correct that Adrian does the firing, and not me, but it's me who my coworkers come to for answers when it's done. All of them are upset, and nothing I can say offers them any comfort.

It's as if my office becomes the place to vent. The place for them to safely unleash their anger. Unfortunately for me, it also appears to be the day the graphics department is getting culled.

So one after the other pass snide looks my way before heading to their office with empty boxes to clear out their things.

They just lost their jobs. I feel compassion for them, even the ones I didn't get along with very well. Frustration mounts and I'm more upset than ever toward the end of the day.

A woman who's just been let go comes into my office at

three. "What the hell, Suzette?" Her face is almost white, and her voice shakes from how upset she is. "Half of the department was just let go."

"He's rearranging things," I say helplessly. "I'm so sorry."

"Let me guess, there's nothing you can do."

"I'm sorry," is my only reply. I can't give her anything else. I'm not the owner of the company; Adrian is, and I'm not even the second step down in the company. "I have no input or authority."

"Wonderful," she says sarcastically. "Goodbye, Suzette."

A few minutes later, another person who has been fired storms across the hall. He turns his head and stares at me on his way past, but doesn't say a word.

It's not until Gail comes back, taking her seat and appearing on the verge of tears. "If you knew something, you would tell me, right?" We've worked together for years and I've never seen her like this. Her tan skin is flushed. "If I'm going to lose my job, I just need to know so—" her voice cracks and I can't take it.

"The second I know anything—"

"Could you ask him?" She stresses, "Please?" Her dark brown eyes are rimmed in red and I know she's a mess witnessing so many layoffs so quickly and with whispers of a merger, where our jobs would no doubt overlap with others and thus, more layoffs.

"Please," she begs me. With a nod, and a tight swallow,

I agree.

"I can ask him," I tell her and then I firm up my response. "I'll ask him today."

Sitting here and waiting for an answer isn't enough, not for me and not for the team members I have left. I've worked far too hard for this company to let it all go to shit like this. If we lose Gail, the report we put together today is irrelevant. Clients stay with us because of the team. We can't break down like this.

I won't let it happen.

At five forty-five, I knock on the door to Adrian's office. Shaking out my hands, I prepare myself. Not the version of me he sees after six. But the version who existed before that man dared to walk through the doors to this building. The badass businesswoman who doesn't take any shit.

It's a small blessing that his secretary is gone for the day and her desk is empty now. Most of the building is cleared out, but not everyone. And I have fifteen minutes. He can offer me fifteen minutes if it means saving the most profitable department in this company.

"Come in," Adrian calls from inside the office.

Steeling myself, I open the door and go in, then close it behind me. The move is fast and I say a silent *thank you* that his door was unlocked.

Before he can say a word, I approach his desk. It seems to take forever and the scent of people's fear as they got fired today hangs in the air. His large, spacious office must have seemed like an awful joke to the people who lost their jobs. I could be one of them, and Adrian is the only one who can confirm my fear or dismiss it. That's why I'm here. This conversation is needed, because I can't sit at my desk for another day with nothing to say to the people I've worked with for years as they file out past me. I handpicked my department. They should be able to rely on me.

"My department is essential to what our company does," I begin, without waiting for his permission. I don't need it outside of the games we play. "If you want to keep the company going, you'll need to keep the core team intact. Every single one of them is essential, and I can vouch for them and their work."

Adrian shifts in his seat, his dark suit crisp, his expression inscrutable. As he leans back, his hands relaxed on the armrests, I wait for any reaction at all, but I'm given nothing.

"Almost everyone I could part with is already gone, and my team won't be able to keep functioning if we lose any more people. We've brought in the most revenue of any other department over the last few years, and you can expect more of the same over the next five years. We're projected to triple our profits by then."

Adrenaline rages through me at the very fact that we will triple in only five years. There's not a damn word I've said that's exaggerated. My heart hammers in my chest as I stare back at Adrian's cool gaze. Again, he doesn't react other than to gesture to continue.

"I'm damn good at my job, and I have good people, and we're going to keep striving for excellence."

"Are you done?" he questions.

"There's no one who can do what we do and keep those clients. No one has the relationships we do. No one has the word of mouth that we do. Replacing any of us would be a mistake."

I swallow so hard, it's audible and still, I'm given nothing.

"Adrian." I whisper his name, on the verge of breaking. Anger simmers but also a hurt I can't describe.

"We're on the clock, Suzette," he warns, the first sign of compassion noted in my name on his lips.

"If you're going to lay them off," I say and swallow, "I need to be able to tell them. I need to know what's going on."

"That's what you came here for? To figure out who's getting fired next?" His tone is unimpressed.

"I want you to keep in mind that we're a team. We work efficiently and our plan is solid; our performance speaks for itself."

He eyes me from across his desk, lips pursed. "You'll have an answer when the team is ready."

Frustrated, I look him in the eye. "You could at least say you'll consider it. You can at least tell me you'll let me know if anyone is in danger."

"I won't. It doesn't matter, Suzette. The team is running the numbers. The numbers are what guide my decision, not emotions. Not a plan, but what has been done and what is comparable. You're aware you have a list of clients, but they aren't the only clients and even that list is sellable."

Heat spreads over the back of my neck. I'm burning with frustration and anger, tears stinging the corners of my eyes. "You're heartless. You know what this means."

"And you know I bought this company for profit, and it's been bleeding money for far too long."

I'm left speechless, staring at him with nothing but resentment.

He won't give in, and somehow it shocks me. I should have known this about Adrian Bradford. He takes what he wants and does what he wants.

I knew that all too well when he fucked me on this desk the very first day we met. My heart hurts and I put my hand up to cover it, but it's too late. The damage is already done. "I can't believe you won't even give me the respect of letting me know if my team is at risk of losing their livelihoods. If you're just going to sell off the list, you could tell me that. I'm not fucking stupid. You would know if you already had a buyer."

Adrian folds his arms over his chest. "I listen because it means something to you. Do you think I would have let anyone else barge in here without a meeting?"

That same sickness from earlier stirs and I say nothing, knowing he's the one who's caused it.

"There needs to be a ... separation for us."

"How the hell am I supposed to separate this?" is all I can

respond, my voice shaky.

"I want you to be happy," Adrian says simply, unfolding his arms and pushing the chair out from his desk slightly. "I want you to know I care for you."

There's a pause, and my frustration grows again. He cares for me? But can't answer a simple question? "They need to know as soon as possible so they can prepare," I press further and Adrian doesn't budge, his lips pressing into a thin line.

"Would you really sleep with me one night and then fire me in the morning?" I question with my voice tight.

"Suzette," he says, his voice carrying a note of warning. He doesn't say no.

Betrayal seems to push out every other feeling I have, making my face hot and my chest hurt. I know a losing argument when I see one and I know Adrian won't be convinced right now, but I can't help myself. "The company—"

"It's after six, Suzette," he replies, cutting me off. "You'll have your answer when the team has consolidated numbers and risks."

"Oh," I say with a bitter tone. "You can't tell me now because you're off the clock. Because it's six, so now I'm just a lowly fuck toy for you to come in?" Even as the words escape my mouth, I know they cross the line.

"You know that's not why." His statement is a string of carefully restrained anger, his grip tightening on the armrests, turning his knuckles white. Good. I hope he's pissed off. I hope he's upset like I am.

"I would never speak to you like that," he continues. "I would never treat you like you didn't matter. You know that," he tells me, his tone softening, his pale blue gaze pinning me. "And I don't like you talking about yourself like that."

"How am I supposed to—"

"You told me you could separate the two—" I cut him off before he can finish.

"I'm trying to compartmentalize," I argue back. He's gripping the desk, obviously upset now. "I'm sorry. I need a moment and I think—" Just as I turn my back to him, ready to get the hell out of here so I can lose it alone in a bathroom stall, he speaks up.

"No. We need to get out of here. We have dinner plans."

How am I supposed to sit through dinner like this with my stomach in knots and my face burning? I don't think I can do it. "Maybe we shouldn't tonight."

All my emotions tumble over me, filling my body and seeming to spill over into the room. Tears fill my eyes, but I don't want to cry in front of Adrian. I don't want to cry here in the office, where we've done so many things and where he keeps chipping away at my department and the company I've worked so hard to build.

"Maybe we shouldn't," I say again weakly, and start to leave.

His voice comes immediately, so deep and commanding that it stops me in my tracks. "Don't you dare walk out that door."

CHAPTER 15

ADRIAN

I'm more than aware that there are employees still in the building. A few might be close enough to hear as Suzette bites out, "What the hell did you just say to me?"

She's visibly upset and spiraling. I've seen it before. A hundred times at least. Crying, cursing, screaming at me. I've been struck more than once.

My skin blazes with both indignation and embarrassment. I don't do squabbles in the office, I don't have shouting matches with employees. Then again, I've never slept with anyone at the office before either. This is why. This is exactly why it was a mistake.

With daggers in her eyes, Suzette stares back at me and

says, "Did you just say, 'don't you dare?'" Her voice is deathly low and her gaze narrowed.

Her breasts rise and fall, peeking through her blouse as she breathes in deeply, stalking back toward me.

"I'd like you to calm down," I say, keeping my tone gentle. The last thing I need is publicity or a lawsuit.

Her eyes widen. "Calm down?" Outrage coats the two words. *Fuck.* I can't do anything right by her. This is a lose-lose situation and she sure as hell knew it when she walked in those doors.

I take in a steadying breath, standing from my seat, my dick hard, needing to fuck the anger out of both of us.

"Suzette." I speak her name as she stalks toward me.

"I am struggling today." Her words are frantic. "Watching coworkers pack up their offices, while others didn't even come in. Do you know how many people have given their notice?"

"Fourteen so far," I answer without hesitation. "Change is difficult, uncertainty is difficult, doing *my fucking job* is difficult," I stress, feeling the frustration rise.

"What am I supposed to tell them, Adrian? Rumors are going around about us and they're coming to me like I'm the one who did this," she starts and before she can continue, I stop her in her tracks. Toe to toe I stand apart from her.

"I am doing my best. If my best isn't good enough, then they can go find better." My words are stern and she acts as if they've struck her. Gripping her hips in both of my hands,

I lower my lips to hers to say, "And if any of them have a problem with the two of us, tell them I want you more than anything. More than this company. More than profit, more than any fucking thing. I want you."

She's silent, her wide blue eyes brimming with a mix of emotions. Her hands on my chest put distance between us, so I take them in my own.

"I want you," I repeat, my voice strained and the words raw. "I want you," I tell her a third time, letting it sink in. "This will all be over soon, and when it is, I will still want you."

"Adrian," she says and my name is a plea on her lips, like I'm begging her for something she can't give me. Panic sets in, something I haven't felt in a long damn time.

She knew this was a possibility. I will vouch for her if something happens, but her résumé is impeccable. She will survive. I'll make sure of it. But I cannot guarantee an entire department. I can't promise her the things she's asking for.

"Tell me you want me."

"Adrian," she whispers and her voice is pained. It's unexpected and feels as if she's struck me. I can't remember a time when I've given her a command and she hasn't obeyed.

Moving my hands to hold her, one spearing through her hair and the other on the small of her back, I whisper in her hair before kissing her temple. "Tell me that you want me and I'll make sure you get everything you need."

All I can hear is the sound of her swallowing. I can't lose

her over something like this. Something so insignificant. *It's significant to her, though.*

"It's after six," I remind her. "Come here, let me fuck the memory of that prick boss out of that pretty head of yours."

"Don't," she warns me and uncertainty clouds my judgment. Every inch of my skin is hot, anxiousness quickening my pulse.

"Let it rest for one more night. I promise your department will be the priority tomorrow." I shouldn't have said that. The second the words are out of my mouth, I know I shouldn't have spoken them.

"You promise?"

And still, I double down at the thought that it's what she needed to hear. "I promise."

She pulls back, staring into my eyes. "You promise? Because I don't think I can take much more of what happened today and as much as—"

"I told you, you have my word." With my pulse hammering, I bend to kiss her, deeply and desperately. I've lost the upper hand and I couldn't care less. Her lips mold to mine, but she's quick to break them.

"I'm sorry," she whispers between us. Picking her ass up, I move her to the desk, her legs spread as I stand between them.

She repeats, "I'm sorry, I shouldn't have come in when I was—"

"Stop," I say and then kiss her again.

"No." She pushes me back, breaking my hold on her and heaving in a breath. "I'm sorry I didn't tell you that I want you too. I do. I do, Adrian, and I'm sor—"

With my finger pressed against her lips, I give her the command, "I said quiet." Heat dances along my skin. Both of us pent up, both of us suffering from the way we came to be.

Working the knot of my tie, I order her, "Lie back, with your hands by my chair."

She doesn't hesitate, eager to make it up to me.

My mind whirls with the implications of what's happened in the last hour, but I can barely focus on anything other than taking back control.

"You'll be quiet," I tell her in a whisper, steadying my breath as I use my tie to form a handcuff knot and stalk around to the other side of the desk. Slipping both of her hands through, I tighten them and then order, "Above your head."

She doesn't object and although the loose end is short, I'm able to tie it to the drawer handle. Lying flat on her back across the desk, her hands above her head, she has to bend her knees so her heels balance on the edge of the desk.

"What am I going to do to you?" I round the desk, loving how she looks.

This is better. This is how she should be.

With a hand on each of her hips, I drag her so her ass is at the edge of the desk. Her gasp fuels me further. Reaching up her skirt, I bunch it and drag her panties down her ass until they're free from her and a pile of lace on the floor.

"Spread your legs," I command and she obeys.

I position her heels how I want them, her legs spread as wide as she can. Fucking gorgeous. Her cunt is right there for the taking. Standing between her thighs, I unbutton her blouse one button at a time, exposing her blush-colored bra. I wish I'd taken it off before I thought to have her lie down. Her breathy pants are additive.

"This is how I want you in this office after hours."

Dipping the cups down, I free each breast, plucking and pinching her nipples and taking my time to play with them.

"My plaything, mewling for me."

"Adrian—"

"You'll be silent or I'll gag you, my little vixen. Do you understand?"

She starts to answer and thinking better of it, she swallows thickly and nods. The cords around her neck tighten, and I lean down, trailing kisses there as my hand slips to her slit.

"So fucking wet already," I murmur against her neck. "My greedy little whore … let's see how much you can take." With my lips on hers, I keep her quiet as I slip two fingers inside of her, curling them and quickly finding the bundle of nerves that has her sucking in a breath and arching her neck. My thumb moves to her clit and I'm ruthless as I force the first orgasm from her. It doesn't take long at all, her heels slipping from the edge of the desk, her muted cries of pleasure silenced as I devour her mouth with my own.

When she clenches around me, I only pause for a moment, wetting a third finger with her arousal before doing it all again. I don't kiss her this time, I stare down at her as she closes her and her head thrashes.

"Adrian." My name is hardly recognizable as it mixes with a tortured cry of pleasure.

Pulling my hand from her I smack her pussy, my middle finger landing directly on her clit.

Her arms pull back, the tie keeping her restrained, and her back bows as she cries out a beautiful sound of desperation.

"Quiet now, my little vixen," I tell her and her darkened gaze finds mine. Once she's regained her composure, I do it again, fucking her with three fingers until she comes undone.

My cock is hard watching her skin flush. When I finally thrust inside of her, I'm not merciful in the least. The desk allows me to fuck her deeply and roughly. Punishingly so.

She thought she was sore two days ago ... she won't be able to walk out of here when I'm done with her.

CHAPTER 16

SUZETTE

The only thing allowing me to calm down last night was, ironically, Adrian. If he hadn't taken me in his office, I don't think I would have been able to sleep. After being taken so thoroughly all I could think about was a hot bath, pajamas, and a glass of wine. My worries couldn't keep me awake long after that and I took my well-fucked body to bed.

A part of me is convinced he only said those things to pacify me. That he told me tomorrow he would give me a straight answer so I would calm down. The other part of me knows he hasn't given me a reason to think he'd lie to me. He's many things, but he hasn't lied to me. All of me, though, every single part of me is embarrassed for losing it on him. It wasn't professional and it crossed the lines we agreed upon.

With all of those thoughts fighting for the center stage of my insecurity, sleep wasn't as restful as I'd hoped it would be. My light dreams were far too real. Coworkers glared at me from outside my office door. No one would tell me what was happening, though. They wouldn't give a reason why they were so angry. "We're transitioning," I said, and I knew it didn't make any difference. Eventually, the dreams stopped and I fell into a deep sleep for all of a handful of hours.

I think it's safe to say the reality of my position at work is catching up to me.

My outfit for today was a decisive choice. It consists of a pencil skirt and blouse that is the epitome of attire for head bitches in charge. Selecting my accessories carefully, I went with classic pearl studs and paired them with a triple strand of pearls.

Giving myself a once-over, I nod. My outfit is perfect, and I'm calm enough from last night to face whatever Adrian says this morning. Although I'm exhausted with bags under my eyes, I'm a professional and I'll act accordingly.

None of it explains how my hands go numb and my stomach turns over every time I think of Adrian, though. This is exactly why they say not to fuck your boss. Every instinct I have tells me that today is our last day and potentially my last day at work as well.

He's taken over my mind and my emotions. How the hell

did I let that happen?

I can lie to myself all I want as I smooth my skirt down, but he's still lingering behind every one of my thoughts.

I reassure myself on the trip into the office that I'll be professional and that whatever happens, I will survive. And that these emotions are warranted. It's perfectly normal to experience insecurities around something as intimate as sex, and something as forbidden as sex with the man who holds your future in his hands. Not just your future, either, but that of everyone you work with.

The thoughts marinate all throughout my morning routine. From paying for my morning coffee at the stand on the corner, to nodding at colleagues on my way to the elevator. These feelings and thoughts don't leave me. Dwelling on it all won't help. All I want to do is rip the fucking bandage off.

My thoughts will only get more complicated, and what can simplify them is answers. The email went out this morning, and four people have already texted me. The only one I replied to was Gail, who's waiting for me so we can head to the conference room together. Three departments are meeting at once this morning. The last three. Just the thought sends unease washing through me again.

"You ready?" Gail asks me, a notebook tucked under her arm as she pulls the hem of her dress down. It's a dark red number with three-quarter sleeves, and it hugs her curves all the way down to her thighs.

Red is a confident color. Nodding, I lift my coffee to her. "Let's do this."

It's quiet as we take the elevator up. "At least we'll know," Gail murmurs and I nod, choosing not to say anything at all. Her nervousness is as obvious as mine.

I hate this. I hate every bit of it and that's all I can think as we settle into the room, all twenty chairs filled and three men standing in the back corner.

The conversation swells from soft murmurs and gossip to one man speaking far too loudly in the room and then all at once stops.

Adrian strides to the head of the table to address everyone. If I hadn't spent so much time with him, knowing the curve of his jaw, the strength in his stance, I might not notice the subtle darkness under his eyes, as if he hasn't slept either.

His suit is crisp, though, custom fitted no doubt, and his shoulders set back, the air seeming to bend around him.

"Good morning," he says, and my body instantly heats. He has all the power to turn our lives upside down, but I still crave the sound of his voice. "I'm not going to waste any time. As part of this company's restructuring, some departments will be dissolved."

Sucking in a breath, I prepare myself.

"Your applications will be suggested to a competitor who will need to hire a number of positions after a merger." His eyes meet mine. "The only department that stays is brand positioning and marketing. It will stay in its entirety."

Mutters fill the room instantly, but Adrian cuts them off with a gesture.

"Did he say our department?" Gail whispers. And I nod without thinking. It's what he said, isn't it? He said brand positioning and marketing?

Gail lets out a not-so-subtle sigh and grabs my hand, squeezing so tight that my knuckles hurt. My department is safe. I can barely breathe, let alone sit here and absorb everything else he said.

There will be a merger.

He said there will be a merger.

We are safe, but what are the details of the merger? What exactly is happening? A split-up? He continues, fielding questions and a few men file out without a single word. They're pissed, dealing with the gravity of the situation. Everything seems to happen around me in a whirl. I have a million questions for Adrian. If the other sectors are being merged, what does that mean for my department? I rely on finance and purchasing and production to do what I do. Our department is all about ideas and relationships, but bringing those ideas to life relies on others. Does this mean I'll have to outsource? To the new company, even?

It's not long before I feel lingering stares on the back of my neck, and my ears go hot. They're all stealing glances at me, one by one. The corners of their mouths are turned down in disapproving frowns.

They know. This looks bad. So fucking bad. And yet, it's what I asked for. The reality of their assumptions hits me.

Everyone here knows I've been sleeping with Adrian, and they think he's keeping my department because I couldn't keep my legs closed. It will never matter to them that I took my own power in being fucked by him. All they see is a woman who went behind everyone's back to sleep with the boss and guarantee her department would stay intact.

That sickening feeling takes over again. Every part of me is on edge and Gail seems to catch on, squeezing my hand again and whispering, "Fuck them."

Frustration clenches my jaw. For so many years, I've thrown myself into this work and made tough calls and spoken my mind to my superiors even though I knew it would be risky to do it. I've been the one on the line many times, all in service of building this company into something worthwhile. Now everyone in the room thinks I slept my way to the top. Not even to the top. They think I slept my way to keeping my job.

My discomfort grows with the silence. I'm not sure what Adrian is waiting for, but no one does anything. No one pretends to have another meeting or rushes out with their cell phone to their ear.

It hits me then, that he's reading the room the same as I am. He knows exactly what they think and why they're all looking at me. Not Gail or anyone else from my department. Only at me. His gaze slips to mine and the back of my eyes prick. I can take it. I'll deal with the fallout and whatever damage is done to my reputation.

Adrian is handsome and stone faced at the front of the room. He's a defensive, arrogant asshole, that's what he is. Adrian has a strong jaw and an even better smile, but the expression he wears now is hardly encouraging.

"Not one of you came to pitch to me," he says finally in a deadly tone, and the room holds its breath. They've been waiting for the release of finally knowing what's going to happen, and now Adrian's dragging it out. "Not a single one of you but the lead for brand positioning and marketing. One of you came to me with a plan, and I may be a heartless prick, but if there is value and a potential profit …" He's looking deeply into my eyes now, in front of all my colleagues. Every eye in the room is on us. "I do consider it."

CHAPTER 17

ADRIAN

Today was less than ideal. I've never felt so conflicted when it comes to business.

Because she's a factor now. The moment the meeting ended, I left first and I'm ashamed to admit, I closed the door to my office to avoid it all. Especially Suzette and all the questions written in her expression in that conference room.

There's not a doubt in my mind word will get out.

Wyatt clears his throat across from me, and I wish I'd canceled this meeting, but in truth, I'd forgotten about it until he walked through the door.

"Whatever's going on, just tell me," he comments from across my desk. A stack of papers, or more specifically, the contract he wants me to sign sits in front of him. To-go bags from a sushi place are in the other lounge chair beside him.

"We don't have to discuss business," he offers. He's dressed in his lucky dove gray suit. He's worn it to every wedding and every business meeting I've accompanied him to. He told me once that it's his lucky charm. But as he fiddles with the thin pale pink tie, he leans forward, and his eyes search mine. "Whatever it is, you can tell me."

"You didn't come here to be my therapist."

"No, but I'm always your friend. Business aside, you look wrecked." He leans back, his tie wrapped up in one fist that lays on his chest. His brow's pinched as he speaks with concern. "Like, is it a chick, is it your parents? What's going on with you?"

"A chick," I utter before I can stop myself and then I hate it. I hate the description. "She's not just some woman."

"Oh shit." Wyatt elongates the words, pushing the contract out of the way to make room for the sushi.

"I'm not hungry," I tell him and he only pauses to tell me, "Look, I need to eat. You pour your heart out, I'll stuff my face. Whatever's left you can have later." The plastic bag crinkles as he digs out his carton of choice. "So, what'd she do?"

"Nothing that I shouldn't have known was coming." It was written on the walls. Before I even stepped foot in this building, without even looking at the security footage to detail employees, I knew Suzette Parks was going to fight me.

It was written on the fucking walls.

"You're going to have to elaborate," he states, opening up a small container of soy sauce. "She cheat on you?"

"No. No. She wouldn't do that."

"Do we hate her? Want to date her? You haven't given me anything at all, so I'm going to need you to fill me in."

I stare across the desk at Wyatt. He's young, a player, never held on to a woman for more than a few weeks. There isn't shit he could tell me that would help in the least.

"You can vent to me," he assures me, separating a pair of disposable chopsticks and giving me an exasperated look. "Whoever she is, she's gotten to you. You were distracted last time I was here; you're obsessed to—"

"I have feelings for her," I admit to him rather than listen to him continue. "I like her ... a lot and because of that, I compromised a business."

The California roll stops midair. "What business?"

Tapping my two fingers on the desk, I point to the door. "This one."

"What do you mean? You okay moneywise? You need help or something? You know my father—"

"I don't—No. No. It's fine moneywise. It's just ..."

"Oh thank God," he mutters, far more relaxed as he leans back with the container in one hand and the chopsticks in the other.

"It's just, I'm taking a risk I wouldn't, if it weren't for her."

"It's not so bad," he says after an exaggerated swallow. "You've done it before," he reminds me.

"And I nearly lost it all before."

"Passion outweighs statistics." He tells me something I've told him years ago. Pointing the chopsticks at me he adds, "You know that."

I can only nod, feeling the anxiousness of this morning come back to me. "She knows what she's doing and I think this would be best for her," I tell him.

"But not for you?" he guesses.

"... It would be much easier to merge, which means she could lose her job, her entire department even. It would mean uncertainty for her."

"So what, you're keeping her out of it?"

"I'm forming a business for her and her department alone. Allowing her to keep the clients while the remainder of the business is merged with another company."

He arches a brow, surprised. "One of your other companies?"

I shake my head. "I'll profit quickly and be done as far as the merger goes. The investment goes into her business, though."

"Does she know that it's her business?"

"She'll find out soon enough."

"Is she ready for that? That's kind of," he says and repositions himself, more serious now. "It's kind of a lot."

"It was that or the alternative, giving her passion to

someone else to control."

Wyatt shakes his head, his brow still raised as if it's stuck there now. "Well okay, so ... now I see why your mind is occupied." He aims for another piece of sushi but stops before picking it up. "Wait, you're screwing someone here?" he questions. "Like you're sleeping with the head of a department and because of that, you're forming a company for her to protect her from the obviously correct business decision?"

My stomach drops as I nod. "More or less."

"How long have you been with her? It's got to be serious."

"Less than a month, but yes. I'm serious when it comes to her."

If I thought his brow couldn't raise any higher, I thought wrong. It's quiet a moment, and the weight of my decision settles against my chest, uncomfortable and heavy.

"So, you're telling me," Wyatt pipes up, chopsticks once again aimed at me, "all I have to do to get you to sign these papers is sleep with you?"

The laughter is unexpected and if there was anything on my desk, I'd toss it at him. It's the first time I've smiled all day. "You're an ass, you know that?"

"I'm an ass who's happy you're in love," he comments and everything stops. "Men in love do stupid things but, if she's worth it, she's worth it."

"She's worth it," I tell him quickly. Ignoring the cold sweat that slips down the back of my neck at the thought of being in love with her.

"Good, maybe marry her or something. In case the company takes off."

"Marriage is not a business deal."

Wyatt shrugs. "It could be."

The knock at my office door is discreet and Andrea reveals herself. "Mr. Bradford, I just wanted to let you know the next meeting is seating now."

"Thank you, Andrea."

"All right, I'll get going then." Wyatt stands to leave. He takes in a deep breath and pushes the contract my way. "While you're a little puppy dog in love, could you take a look at that and sign it, please?"

Picking up the contract, I tell him, "You got it." I decide then and there that I'll sign it tonight.

Andrea watches our exchange from the threshold of the door.

"Give me five, and then can you scan this in for me?"

"Of course," she says warily and I look up at her.

"Everything all right?"

"Just checking on you. I know things are a bit tense at the moment."

"It's nothing I haven't dealt with before."

She stares back, her glasses slipping slightly from the bridge of her nose and her brow rises just as Wyatt's did. "Is there something else? Something you want to say?"

She shakes her head softly, the corners of her lips turning down. "No, sir."

"You can tell me," I say. "If there's something on your mind, speak freely."

"If Ms. Parks asks to meet with you, would you like me to let her up still?"

"Of course," I'm quick to answer.

"Good, good." Relief colors her face.

"Why would you ask?"

"She seemed upset yesterday, and so did you this morning. I just ... I'm glad to hear that, is all."

CHAPTER 18

SUZETTE

Guilt and nervousness and gratefulness spin through my mind for the rest of the day at work. All I can do is count down the minutes until 6:00 p.m. when I know Adrian will step into that elevator and I can be raw with him and let everything out. It's a gray area regarding the boundaries we set, but I have to get it out of me.

It's a mix of every emotion, so intense I have trouble concentrating on anything at all. My office door stays closed and I ignore every text and email and knock. I rescheduled several meetings and give myself the day to gather my composure.

This is what I wanted. It's exactly what I was hoping he would tell me was going to happen when I stormed into his office yesterday. Keeping my department whole is security and yet I feel nothing but insecure.

It all feels wrong. Just then my inbox pings with a new email notification and the subject line encompasses exactly what plays on repeat in my mind: *If you weren't sleeping with him, you'd have to fight for your job like the rest of us after the merger.*

There's a sinking feeling in my chest and when I click on the email header, the address is one I don't recognize. More than likely it's a throwaway account.

"Fuck you," I mutter and click delete although I can't say that they're wrong.

For the last hour, I do what I can, making plans for reassuring our clients and reaching out to other department heads to ensure we have what we need to continue.

If we don't, we will. I won't let us miss a beat. It's critical for our clients to know we're stable and there won't be any delays.

If Adrian is keeping our entire department, I have to make sure we have something to show for it. We have to be the best, now that he's singled us out.

I feel guilty that my department is staying because of what Adrian and I have done together ... but not guilty enough to stop doing it.

I'm nervous that he'll change his mind and even more nervous that he'd be right to do it. And I'm grateful to him for announcing in front of everyone that he would be keeping our department. It saves me an untold amount of time trying to reply to questions when I don't have any firm answers.

I shake off the nervousness as best I can when it's finally time to get into the elevator. The office has been emptying out for a while now, and there's no one to see me step in. Adrian is already there waiting, occupied with his phone. When he glances up at me, my heart races. All the jitters rev up and I forget everything I was going to say.

"I can't do dinner tonight. I have a number of things that have piled up and arrangements that need to be finalized." My heels click as I step into the elevator, pretending like that's all right. Like it doesn't feel as if he's struck me and confirmed that everything is wrong and off between us.

"Okay," I say softly, staring straight ahead as the doors close.

"I can drop you off at your place if you'd like," he says briskly. It's cold and I stand a little further away from him as the elevator moves. He puts his phone in his pocket and presses the button for the first floor.

"Are we okay?" Now what I'm feeling is all nerves. It's tense between us, and different. There's none of the hot playfulness that's been part of every meeting we've had, and I can't help but wonder if it's because of what he did earlier. I know Adrian made that choice because of me. Guilt comes roaring back.

Adrian lets out a sharp breath and punches the emergency stop button on the elevator. "I need us to be—" he begins, and then he grabs me, pulling me commandingly across the space and into his arms. He lifts my face to his and kisses me hard and passionately, his tongue seeking entry into my mouth, and I part my lips for him with a moan. Heat blazes between us in an instant. It's unexpected but oh so needed.

Relief and desperation stir inside of me as I cling to him. My back hits the wall of the elevator and everything else slips away, fading to black and blurring into nothing.

My breathing is chaotic and my eyes stay closed as Adrian pulls back. His plea is what forces my eyes open. "What do you need from me to prove to you that you matter to me? That I want you happy and I want you mine and I couldn't give two shits about anything else?"

Gripping his collar, my fingers grazing against his stubble, I selfishly pull him in for another kiss, soft, slow and deliberate. He tastes minty and every bit of the man I know him to be. I could live here in this elevator if it meant kissing him forever.

Staring back into his pale blue gaze, I stop myself from the response that begs to be heard. The words are on the tip of my tongue. *I love you, Adrian.* Instead, I kiss him again, needing the stability of his body, until he pulls back to catch his breath. "Will you text me tonight when you're done?" I attempt to make it sound casual, but I'm not sure if it works. "I'm sorry I'm so needy right now."

He takes my face in his hands and looks me in the eye. "Stop saying you're sorry. I will text you." Adrian leans down and presses a kiss to my cheek. "Do you want Noah to take you home?"

I shake my head. "I can spend the evening with Maddie."

Adrian reaches for another button on the elevator's panel, and then we're moving down again. He kisses me all the way to the bottom. "I'll text you," he promises again. One more kiss and the elevator doors open. Adrian is completely self-possessed and put together by the time he steps out of those silver doors and disappears into the lobby.

If only I could be the same.

Maddie's apartment is a cute, small place in SoHo. By small, I mean teeny tiny. It's a one bedroom with a decent-sized living room. A crocheted blanket from her grandmother rests on the back of her sofa and our takeout containers are spread out on the coffee table. The comparison of her place to Adrian's is unavoidable. They are complete contrasts. From the view to the flooring, even the light fixtures. All Maddie has is a single lamp in the corner and ceiling lights in the kitchen. Maddie's fridge hums in the little kitchen off the living room and every so often the radiator makes a clicking sound. Even if it is small, it's comforting to be here. It reminds me of when I first moved here. Before my ex, before this job. Over a decade ago now.

Curled up on the other side of the couch, Maddie works

her way through the Chinese I picked up on the way here and groans about her latest hellish dating experience.

"He wanted me to pay for everything, including his dinner, after he was such a dick because, quote unquote, 'If you don't want to see me again, that's on you and you wasted my time,'" she says. Her eyes widen just as mine do, with disbelief. "I shit you not."

"That is ... exceptionally ... like, I don't even have words."

"I would have been happy to split the bill, but are you kidding me? I'm not going to pay a fee for not liking the guy."

"That sounds awful," I say, commiserating. "It's bullshit that you even have to put up with guys like that."

"I don't," Maddie tells me and laughs. "I left him in that restaurant. I just wish there were more good guys on this freaking app, you know? It's so exhausting to have to search through all of them. Like I'm obviously not good at picking, could someone else do it for me?" A titter leaves her, but I know she's less than happy and there's truth to the statement.

"I haven't looked at a dating app in a long time now." Stirring the lo mein with my fork, I add, "Not for ... months now?" I surmise, "Not since those first few weeks of the separation."

Chewing my inner cheek, I keep my next thoughts to myself. I never would have found a man like Adrian on an app. My throat is tight with how much I miss him, and how I want things to be normal between us. It's been a long damn time since I've missed someone. Truly missed them, and that realization toys with me as well as Adrian himself does.

"Men are trash," Maddie says and sighs, and that's what does it.

I break down crying over my Chinese food. What the hell is wrong with me? "I swear I better be getting my period or something because I am nothing but an emotional wreck today." I create the excuse, pushing it out the moment I lose it. The small napkins from the restaurant make for perfect tissues.

"Oh my God." Maddie places her container onto the coffee table and scoots over next to me, slinging an arm around my shoulders. "What happened? It's okay to cry," she tells me. Of course she would say that. She's the emotional one. I'm not. This isn't me. It's not who I am.

"You know about Adrian," I barely manage to get out. "You heard the gossip at lunch, and you know what those rumors say and you know it's true but ... it's not just sex."

Maddie's eyes are wide. She keeps giving me little nods, like she's following along, but when the pause comes her mouth drops open. She cracks a bright smile. "It's not just sex? Is it—"

"No," I cut her off. "It's more than that." Another sob wracks me and it only frustrates me more. "I think I'm falling for him."

CHAPTER 19

ADRIAN

Sitting in the office, overlooking the city, I come to one conclusion. There's only one reason I would negotiate everything like I have the past three days. Every meeting, the marketing department and client list was mentioned. Every deal, the number went up, with the condition it was included in the acquisition of the company ... and I turned all of them down. Settling for less. Barely breaking even on a deal I spent months pursuing.

It was all to her and compromising every other deal.

Of course they took what I offered, though. Everyone who needed to sign, did so. Ending the majority of their competition was a worthwhile deal for them. Even if the coveted list remains with Suzette. Her job is secure. It will be unsteady for a while I imagine as she adjusts. She will, though, she will survive and she will thrive. There's no doubt in my mind, even from the numbers' side, and the team agrees. It's not cost-effective and it's a risk to float the company, but for her, knowing that there's not a chance in hell her position will be in jeopardy, it's worth it.

And there's only one conclusion I can make of that. It would have been a quick few million, freeing up my cash flow, ending one project and moving on to the next. Instead, I'll be supporting a company who may lose clients, whose stock will plummet once the split is finalized. A company that will have to prove themselves ... a company run by her.

I think I love her.
I think I want to propose to her.

My phone rests in my lap and I stare down at the messages I typed out. I delete the two texts. It's insanity. Running my hand through my hair, I groan at the ridiculousness of it all.

I haven't a clue how Suzette will even react once reality hits her. I've gifted her a company. Technically the board will meet and vote on the positions needed to be filled to move forward. She will be nominated and everything she worked for, will come to fruition.

Heat tingles along my skin, not knowing how she will

take it.

The meeting is set for next week and my instinct screams to secure her before then. To propose, to woo her, so that when the time comes and it dawns on her, she'll already be mine.

All of that doubt and insecurity will be worthless if she's already wearing my ring.

It's one thing for a man infatuated to shower a lover with wealth, a lover with trust issues and one that seems to be ready to run any minute. It's another for a future husband to secure his fiancée's livelihood.

The only question that remains is whether or not she'll say yes. Whether she wants me like I want her.

I'm infatuated. I've lost my fucking mind over her.

I think I'll propose to her. I type it out to Wyatt and wait a moment, debating on whether I should do it without telling anyone. I could take her to any jewelry store she wanted, let her choose the ring she wants most and do it then and there.

My thumb hovers over the message.

I already know Wyatt is going to try to talk me out of it. That's what I would do, if he texted me out of nowhere that he wanted to propose to a woman he just met last month.

A woman who's gotten into his head and clouded everything.

But isn't that what love is?

I don't have a moment to send it. Wyatt and my father message me at once.

Wyatt's message asks if he can see me.

He adds: *It's important. As soon as you can, I need to see you.*

An anxiousness comes with my father's message: *You didn't sign that contract, did you?*

My gut drops and Wyatt messages: *Where are you? I'll come to you now. I fucked up. It's all fucked up.*

There's a prick at the back of my neck, a numbness that flows through my veins.

I respond to them both immediately.

To my father: *I signed it.*

To Wyatt: *At the office.*

My father: *Fuck. Call me now.*

Wyatt texts back at the same time that my father calls. Clearing my throat, I glance at the closed office door and then turn my back to it, facing the office windows.

"Adrian." My father greets me and before I can do the same he says, "Tell me you didn't sign it."

"I already told you I did."

The tone in his voice is unsettling, enough so that my entire body tenses. There's desperation I can't help but to feel pulling at me through the line.

"Whatever he's gotten himself into, I'll help him out."

"It's not just him," my father grits out between his teeth. "Did your lawyers not change the fucking clause? You're on the hook for his investment in the building."

"What?" My pulse races and I'm quick to open up the

drawer, pulling out an unsigned copy, a previous version Wyatt had given me. Andrea has the signed copy. Signed, sealed, delivered.

"He made the purchase this weekend for the real estate not two days before the city announced the fucking highway would be built across the street."

Wyatt's deal, his big idea, was high-end residential builds. It's what his father made his name doing. They're builders and damn good. "A highway?" I can't fucking believe it. "How did he not know?"

"The more important question is, how the fuck does he sell it now and how the hell do you get out of this contract? If not, you're going to have to sell as much as you can. It's to the tune of twenty million."

"Twenty million," I repeat, bracing myself on the desk. The numbers run in my mind, all of the companies, all of the holdings and deals I could maneuver just to cover a short like that.

"Twenty fucking million." Every way I look at it, one company stands out above the rest. Worth eight million for a single client list.

I could fucking throw up.

"You'll sell if you have to, hold on to the best investments only. I'll help where I can, but I don't see a way out. You're going to have to shift money and hold out for the right timing."

"I need at least a hundred grand a month for a different investment." All the numbers for payroll and transitions tally in my mind. The company will earn it back, but not in the first quarter. Probably not for the first year. It has to float.

"For what?" My father's tone is exasperated. "You'll be lucky if you have enough for your personal expenses."

"I'll leave those numbers to my financial manager," I bite out, irritated but also fucking terrified. I saw what happened to my family years ago when my father lost it all.

As if reading my mind he states clearly, "You might be fucked, but you'll survive this. You're going to have to sacrifice a number of things, but I'm calling the lawyers, I'm calling everyone. I will do everything I can, but I'm not sure there's much we can do but sell. Take the hit. Reinvest when there's time. At least it's only twenty million lost."

I can barely swallow, my eyes closed as I realize what I would do if things were different. A quick eight million is right there.

"Fuck," I say and breathe out. I promised her. I promised her she didn't have to worry.

"I can't fucking believe I signed."

"I can't believe he was that fucking stupid."

"It's his first on his own."

"Even still, he should have fucking known to talk. He could have made fucking sure there weren't whispers and deals in the making. If he'd told his father, at the very least, he could have been given a heads-up."

Investors talk. Politicians are paid. Deals are made. It's

how this business is run. But only those in certain circles are privy to high-level information. Wyatt's father would have known. He would have stopped him from buying property whose value was days away from plummeting.

"If the sellers knew—"

"Do you know how long litigation would take? And that's if you can prove it." I swallow thickly. There's a reason they say the business world is run by crooks.

He got fucked over. And I signed the dotted line to come along for the ride.

Just then, the office door opens, Andrea calling out behind Wyatt.

With my phone pressed to my ear, my father cursing and repeating lines of the contract. Wyatt stares back at me, his eyes rimmed in red and looking like hell. His light tan skin is blotchy like he's barely keeping it together.

"I fucked up. It's a lot of fucking money."

"Sir," Andrea starts, a nervous energy around her.

"It's fine, Andrea." I wave her away as Wyatt takes hesitant steps inside the barren office, his hand running down his face. "I'll call you back," is all I say to my father without taking my eyes off my good friend, who just made a horrific deal ... one for the both of us.

Chapter 20

Suzette

I knock softly at Adrian's door and go in. It's the latest I've ever visited him, but he's been busy all day and evening. As it stands I've barely seen him the last two days, and when I do, he's reserved with me and soft in a way he hasn't been before. I nearly left, thinking maybe he just needed space and wasn't telling me, but I thought better of it.

I messaged: *I have work I can do too, do you mind if I stop by later tonight?*

His response told me everything I needed to know: *I'd love it if you did.*

So with all these nerves still wreaking havoc inside of me, and the realization that I'm head over heels for a man and I think he may be head over heels for me too, I crack open the door to his office.

"Adrian," I call out, saying his name as if to gauge whether or not he's done even though he told me if I came up at nine he should be finished.

Sitting at his desk, Adrian runs his hands over his hair. "Suzette," he responds, my name a murmur on his lips. His stress is apparent even from the door.

"Come have a drink with me," he offers and I instantly relax.

I go around his desk and fold my arms around him from behind, resting my chin on his shoulder. He leans into me for a kiss on the cheek and I feel like I could burst with all the things that threaten to spill out of me. There are so many things that I can't decide what to say first. That I love him? That I'm in love with him? It feels almost childish, raw and vulnerable. It doesn't escape me that I'm insecure and he hasn't given me a reason not to be. I'm holding back and he hasn't as far as I know. This is the part of the relationship where it doesn't feel even.

He may be my boss, the devil in a suit, rich and powerful and I'm lowly compared to him on the surface of it all, but I've never felt inferior. Not until now. Not until I've realized how I feel and that I'm terrified to admit it, just in case he doesn't feel the same.

Adrian turns his face to mine and stands up, pushing his chair out of the way before I can speak. I can taste alcohol on him. He's been drinking, no doubt to get rid of the stresses of the day, though it's a good stress. At least I thought it was. The numbers are good and I'm excited for our meeting next week. I'm not sure what it will entail but I already have a business plan laid out. It'll be wonderful, I can reassure him of that.

"I need you," he whispers against the crook of my neck and the warmth of his breath forces my head to fall back and desire spreads through me like wildfire.

He's almost frantic at my clothes, pushing my skirt up and lifting me onto the desk. A gasp leaves me and it's all too welcomed. Maybe he needs this as much as I do. Adrian strips off my panties with an efficient movement as he looks me in the eyes, his emotions running through them too fast for me to name them all. He undoes his belt and zipper and pushes into me with the same ferocity he used that first day. He's not shy about putting his hands on my body wherever he wants them. He touches me everywhere he can reach, with a firm grip on my thighs and my hips. Adrian fucks me in the way I love him to, with possessive strokes. Pleasure pools between my legs at how close he is and how intimate it is to be used like this.

My nails dig into his shoulder as I moan his name. His thrusts are merciless and the pleasure builds and builds without warning.

We're in danger of knocking things off the desk now and it's so hot to see him unraveling like this.

All too soon, I come first and then he follows. It's only when he leaves me, both of us still catching our breath that I realize he's fully clothed.

"Would you want me still if I couldn't afford it?" His question came out of nowhere.

"What?" My head is cloudy with lust and my legs still tremble as I try to gather what he's said. "Afford what?"

"To support the split. To fund the company during the changes."

I pull back so I can look into his eyes, following his movements as he undoes his tie and then reaches into his desk for tissues, no doubt to clean up. I'm surprised that he's talking business after six, let alone the second he finished inside of me. Of all the things I want to respond, I want to tease him about it, to lighten it and allay any worries he has.

Before any words can leave me, his gaze pins me. It's one of a wounded man. The same vulnerability that plagued me all day stares back at me.

"I couldn't give two shits if you have money. I don't care." The last couple of days play through my mind. "Is that what's been bothering you?" I ask. "Is it because of my department? I mean it, Adrian." I lick my lips, rushing my words out and praying he understands just how much I mean it. "If you don't want to save the department, if it has to go ... I would still want you."

His pace has slowed, but it's as if he can't bring himself to end this conversation. Adrian looks down and I swallow hard.

"Adrian. I swear to you. If you need to tell me something, it's okay." Reaching for the box of tissues and taking it from him, I attempt to convince him. "If you need to tell me something, you can." There's an ache that starts in my chest, but it works its way outward. "I'll still want you."

His pale blue eyes come back to mine again. "Suzette."

"Jobs come and go." I get a lump in my throat from unshed tears and my love for him. *How did this even happen?* I've never wanted to cover myself more, but I'm on his desk and my clothes are on the floor. "Just like clients. I love my job. I love what I do, and I believe in it. But if something were to happen ..." Feeling his eyes on my naked body like this makes me even more emotional. Adrian is so connected to this job for me. I met him here, even though he came to change everything. I don't know whether I'm just clinging to those memories or if I'm genuinely afraid to lose my job. "If funding fell through ..." He doesn't react at all, other than to pull my hips to the edge of the desk and rest his forehead against mine. "If it all fell to shit and was taken away ..."

"Hush."

I do hush, because I can tell what he wants right now is to lose ourselves in the pleasure of this moment.

"I need you again," he whispers and I'm shocked as he pushes me back. Still hard, still demanding and as rough as he was earlier.

"I want you and I'll always want you," he tells me between thrusts, his voice thick with emotion. My lips crash against his and a wave of emotion spreads through me.

I want to tell him, "That's all that matters." But words fail me and strangled moans are all I can offer him.

He groans, "I need more of you."

I spread my legs wide for him and brace my hands on the desk so he can fuck me as hard as he likes. "Come for me," he whispers in my ear, and heat explodes between my thighs in clenching pulses that make him groan and pulse. When he's finished he pulls me off the desk and into his chair. I'm straddling him now, his hands on my waist, and I try to catch my breath so I can continue our conversation.

Even if he doesn't want to. Even if it means being too open, too raw, too needy. I just need him to know exactly how I feel.

"Listen to me." I take his hand and put it to my chest. "I would survive. I could start my company from scratch. I might not be able to keep the clients, but I would find more. I don't want you because you can support me, if that's what you're worried about. I want you for you. God knows I hated the idea of you when I first saw you but I—" I swallow, and chicken out, backing away from the truth I'm too scared to voice. "I want you." It's all that I can say.

It's true. If I learned one thing from my divorce, it's that I'll always be able to find a way to support myself. I might worry about it but if the occasion arises, I'll handle it. That's what it means to be a woman in the world. You always have to be able to find a way.

I put both my hands on the sides of his face. "Are you all right?"

He strokes my cheek. "It was only a question. I didn't mean to make you worry."

"If I should worry, you would tell me, wouldn't you?"

He looks deep into my eyes and pulls me in for another kiss. This one is deep and slow and it's like he wants to memorize every part of me. "You don't have to worry," Adrian whispers against my lips. "I want you."

"I want you too." I pull his lip between my teeth and add a little pressure so he can feel it. His deep groan is everything I needed to hear.

Adrian's already hard beneath me again, so it takes nothing to lift myself up and ease back down on his thick length. It's a sweeter connection this time, though he's just as possessive with me. I lean down and kiss him while we move together. Adrian can't help but take control, making his thrusts deeper and harder, and it feels so good that it brings on another orgasm. It moves through my body and makes me tip my head back with the kind of ecstasy I've been looking for all this time for so long. I never thought I'd find it again and I found it here in Adrian. Here in this most forbidden of arrangements.

When it's over I open my eyes and look into his. He's

watching me with heat in his expression and love too. "I love you," I tell him.

He groans and pulls me down onto his cock, fucking me as deep as he ever has. He holds on tightly, as if he never wants to let me go, but he doesn't say it back.

CHAPTER 21

ADRIAN

"The penthouse in Tribeca is five million," I speak clearly, standing in the office and imagining how this office in the high-rise could easily double for temporary housing. I'll take the meetings in the conference room. "I'll sell the furniture with it, that should bring it up another million."

"Business shouldn't affect your personal—"

"We tallied the numbers with the other assets," I repeat to my father. My financial advisor is on the phone as well. He's seen the contract, he knows what deals went down. More importantly, he has a tally of every investment I have. I simply can't lose the majority of them. If I sell now, I'll lose so much more than the current value. There is only so much that can give. "I'll find somewhere cheaper, and that's far better than losing investments or paying the interest."

My financial manager, Sean, speaks through the line, "I agree and there are plenty of other markets on the upswing. It could be beneficial in the long run."

"There's no reason not to sell the list and dissolve the—" My father attempts to chime in. If I didn't respect him as much as I do, I'd tell him to fuck off. To get off the line. To get out of my business. But as it stands, he's my father. He's just as involved in this deal as he has been in the others. He's my mentor and I know he means well. That list and Suzette's departments are nonnegotiable.

I told her I would protect her. And I meant it.

"Yes, there is."

"I saw the deals, Adrian. Why the hell are you doing this? I didn't raise you to—"

"Because she'll hate me," I bite out, forming a fist as my muscles coil. "This is a business call. If you cannot remain professional, I will take the call alone as I would have preferred to do."

"Who is she?"

"It's personal. I'm keeping that investment and I want you to respect that."

"It's worth you losing your home?"

"It's worth me losing everything." The amount of rage is equal to my desperation. Chaos swarms in my blood. "I cannot lose her."

There's silence on the line before an awkward cough from my advisor. Sean states the numbers we've gone over a hundred times in the last six hours.

"If she would hate you for it, then she's not the one for you." My father's tone is somber and before I can say anything else, there's a click on the line.

"Adrian?" Sean questions, "Are you still there?"

"Yes, it was my father who left." There's a hollowness in my chest that fills with a mix of emotions. "Where were we?" I say and then sit back down in the chair.

The money, the power—none of it means anything if I can't have her.

Keeping Sean on speaker, I text my father: *She doesn't know any of this and I don't want her to. I love her and you will too when you meet her.*

I know it's the right thing to do by her. I can make this work. I can have it all.

I text him again before he responds. *Maybe hate was strong. She would be upset, but she wouldn't hate me. I want to do everything I can for her. You need to trust me on this.*

All she needs is this chance. I believe in her and I'll make the money back. I'll be a man worthy of a woman like her.

I just don't know how to tell her or if I even should.

"If we could touch base about the article today," my advisor starts, "it does not seem to be as telling as we were led to believe." I was given a heads-up yesterday that Wyatt's dealing would make headlines. It's a scandal in the making given how the property deal went down.

"I was able to pull some strings," I tell him.

"Have you gotten any pushback from investors? Any concerned calls?"

"A few." My brow pinches at remembering the early calls and emails this morning, wanting to know whether or not the deals would still be going through. "As far as I know, everyone is satisfied."

"Excellent. I know this isn't ideal, but this is manageable. I do, however, recommend not signing any contracts of that magnitude until the lawyers have approved. I spoke with Carly and she told me she had not finished negotiations."

I can only nod, remembering how light I felt, signing that contract … with Suzette on my mind. With Wyatt's approval, about her. Coming to terms with how I'd fallen for her.

"I was distracted," I admit to him.

"Whatever it was, see to it that this doesn't happen again. There's only so much we can do and next time it may not be salvageable."

The knock at my door is hesitant and then Andrea opens it without waiting for a response. It comes at the same time that a text comes through.

"Not now," I tell Andrea who nods and closes the door softly.

I thought it would be my father, but it's Suzette.

I want you. I love you for you. I don't need your money, and I wouldn't think less of you if you weren't in the position you're in.

As if this day could get any harder. I know she loves me. And I'm going to prove to her that I love her back. Words aren't enough.

"It will be tight for a few months unless something breaks. We can file for a few extensions. It will get you through and we can keep it discreet, but you do not have leverage to spend for the time being."

"I understand." A heat tingles the back of my neck. This position I'm in is less than ideal. I can't blame Wyatt. The blame squarely falls on my shoulders.

Sean twists the knife even more. "For all intents and purposes, you are broke."

"I know, Sean. I know what it means."

There's another knock on my door, more forceful than before.

"Mr. Bradford," Andrea speaks up and her tone makes it evident that whatever it is, it needs to be said now.

"I'll call you back shortly," I tell Sean and hang up before he can respond as Andrea walks in. The door closes behind her. Dressed in loose gray pants and a billowy white top, she's nothing but professional.

"What is it?" I question.

"I made a mistake," she tells me, not taking the seat she stands behind.

"We all do," I say, attempting to ease any worries she has, but her expression doesn't appear to reflect that. There's not a worry line in sight.

"The error in the contract with Mr. Wyatt Patton's—" she starts.

I still, my blood going cold. "What about it? What error?"

"I sent in half of the contract signed, but the second half ... Somehow," she says and gestures in the air, a shrug rolling from her shoulders, "I faxed it over unsigned." Her lips quirk up at the end. As if she knows.

Of course she does.

"Andrea." My head falls into my hands for only a moment, the relief waning as if this isn't real. "Could you repeat that, please?" I swallow thickly, praying that what I heard her say is exactly what she did say.

"From what I can tell," she tells me, now taking the seat slowly, "I must have had some questions and somehow I mixed up the paperwork."

"I have to call my lawyer," I tell her, still in a state of disbelief, my hands nearly trembling. If she's serious, if she didn't send it ... It's twenty million that she saved me.

"I thought you might say that." She pats the desk before standing. "She distracts you, but like I've always told you, I've got your back."

"I could kiss you—"

"Please don't," she says jokingly.

"I don't know how to repay you," I tell her softly before she can leave, still not truly believing. Not until I see it myself and not until it's confirmed.

CHAPTER 22

SUZETTE

I don't think I've ever been so nervous for a dinner date. This man has fucked every part of me, he's seen me break down and punished me in ways a younger me wouldn't understand.

He knows me and every inch of me. And that's what scares me. He could crush me so very easily and it would take far more than a bottle of rosé at Maddie's to get over him.

In the back of his car, with Adrian's driver taking me through the city, I sit alone. According to Noah, he's to take me to dinner and Adrian is meeting me there.

I play it off as if I'm not nervous at all. As if tonight doesn't feel different. As if that's a perfectly normal thing to happen. It's a perfect New York City evening. The sunset is a watercolor painting above the buildings, slowly growing darker as the few stars we can see appear high above us.

I'm in love with him, and no matter what he says, I think he loves me too. My heart beats faster with every minute that passes on the drive, and I can't concentrate on my phone. Finally, I put it in my purse and ignore it completely. All the emails I need to send can wait.

I don't miss Noah's eyes peeking back at me and the third time I meet them, I cave.

"Is he going to break up with me?" I question, my voice squeakier than I'd have liked, though I know he's not the person I should be asking.

His head tilts a bit and if I'm not mistaken, the wrinkles that form around his eyes indicate that he's smiling although I can't see that part of his face. "I didn't think you were dating, Ms. Parks."

I laugh, feeling a little less nervous. "Very funny." My fingers fidget among themselves.

He laughs back at me. "He would be a fool to do such a thing. And Mr. Bradford isn't a fool." I can only nod in agreement although I don't feel entirely reassured.

"Besides, we're here so it's a little too late to run."

Peeking out through the tinted window, my gaze focuses on a tempting man in a suit. Heat flows through me seeing Adrian's waiting for me on the sidewalk. He pulls the door open for me before I know what's happening. I step out, slipping my hand into his to keep my balance.

"I'll take it from here," he tells Noah, and that's when I see we're at the Waldorf again. Glancing down at my office attire, I give Adrian a look and he only smirks back.

"If you'd like to go shopping first," he offers although I'm certain it's more for comic relief than anything else.

"You are a devilish man," I comment, and move to stand beside him, his hand still holding mine.

His rough chuckle is a soothing balm. "You look gorgeous," he reassures me.

With every step, the nervousness lingers but it's different now that I'm with him. Maybe it's the way he holds me, or the way he peers down at me. The way his hand splays against my back as we walk in or how he helps me into the booth. I'm not sure what it is, but I want it all.

I would give him everything I have today, for him to simply want me tomorrow.

ADRIAN

"Sir, another?" the waiter asks, politely gathering my attention. If I recall correctly, he's the same waiter we had our first night at the Waldorf, our dinner that never came to be.

The same tucked away booth as well.

I shake my head once. "Thank you, though."

"And for you?" he asks Suzette.

"I'd like dessert I think," she says and gazes back at me as if asking if I'd like to join her.

I only smile back, feeling the nerves heat.

"Maybe the dark chocolate tart?" the waiter suggests and I pray I don't show my reaction in the least.

When the plate comes out, her diamond will be on it. My composure threatens to break when she agrees.

I've gone over every response she could have.

If she says it's too soon, I'll respond, if not now, then when?

If she thinks I've gone crazy, I'll agree, I am losing it because of her.

It doesn't matter what she thinks of it, so long as she says yes. So long as she's mine to have and to hold, to be with me forever. For fuck's sake, if she thinks it has to do with work, I'll tell her how I signed a damn contract I shouldn't have because I couldn't get her off my mind. That alone should convince a businesswoman like her that she should say yes before I go broke drowning in thoughts of her all day.

"Are you all right?" Suzette questions and it's only when I look up to see her glancing at the cocktail napkin in my hand that I realize I've twisted and pulled and creased it to death.

"Fine," I answer her and in my periphery I see the waiter slipping the plate down in front of her.

My heart races and I tell her that I'm perfectly fine and wait.

Her gaze doesn't leave mine. Even when I motion to her dessert, spotting the four-carat diamond sparking from where it sits in the red velvet box.

"I just—" Suzette starts and then licks her lips. "I know I'm ... I know that I—" she hesitates. This gorgeous, intelligent, strong-willed woman hesitates, because of me.

Because I didn't say *I love you* back. I know damn well that's why.

"I want you to marry me," I murmur, unable to hold it back any longer.

Her kissable lips part and her light blue eyes widen. "Adrian."

I motion to the ring on her plate and she gasps, a loud yelp of a gasp, covering her mouth and jumping back slightly.

She stares at it, as if I'm not waiting, unable to breathe and desperate for her to answer me.

"Marry me," I tell her, a command this time and that gets her attention. Her hands lower, although she still stares at me as if she's in shock.

"For the love of all things holy, if you don't say yes right now, I swear to God I'll throw you over this table."

When she smiles, this beautiful smile that reaches all the way up to her eyes, I know it'll be all right.

"I love you," she tells me, her cadence soothing.

"That isn't a yes and I'm going to need you to say—"

"Yes," she says in a breathy voice and it takes everything in me not to topple the table as I rush to her.

To kiss her. To hold her. "I love you too," I tell her the moment she breaks our kiss. "I love you and I need you with me."

Her eyes shine back with every emotion I feel stirring inside of me.

"I love you and I want you, and I need you too."

Epilogue

Suzette

The city never sleeps. It provides a constant light as it slips into the office. Even at nearly 1:00 a.m.

With a deep breath in, I lie back, nestling beside Adrian on the pullout sofa. His smell surrounds me, fresh and clean with a hint of sandalwood, and so do his arms as he wraps them around me, planting a kiss on my forehead.

This is how we've slept for the last two weeks nearly. He stays with me, working and taking calls, while I do the same.

The numbers are promising, but not guaranteed.

"Was it a good day?" he asks me, his chest rumbling as his hand runs down my back.

"A great day. Gail secured the final client."

"That makes me happy to hear," he comments and although exhaustion coats his tone, I know he truly is happy. It was shaky at first. A number of clients debated on leaving, and they all wanted to renegotiate. Gail took the brunt of it.

"Me too," I say and then ask him, "And what about you? Any updates from Wyatt?"

His friend got into a bad deal. I'm not certain of the details but I know it's been rough on him and it involves politicians and a lawsuit and some other developer.

I was nervous at first that it might involve my friend's husband, Mason. He's a developer and I've heard whispers about the depths of corruption that surround him and his family.

He loves Jules, though, and she swears he's one of the good ones. Thankfully, he wasn't involved.

"He'll be all right, but the next few years will be difficult for him. The loan I gave him will help, but he's in for a hellish year if not longer."

"And what about the contract?" Again, the details are murky, but I know at some point, Adrian had signed on to some piece of this shit show.

"It's null and void. Even if I'd signed, he said it was his mistake, we'd never discussed it and he would deal with the fallout."

"He's a good friend."

"He's a good man. Not everyone survives the lows, but he will."

"You still seem down," I comment.

"Just a long day," he says and settles higher up on the bed, "and my little whore has been ignoring me at work."

"It's after six, we're not supposed to talk about work," I tease him, sitting up slightly to nip his bottom lip. He gives me a gruff groan and I love it.

"Hey," I whisper and nudge my nose against his, "I want you."

He hums, that sound I crave before giving me the command, "Roll over."

Heat rushes to my cheeks and I do as he says, laying on my stomach and watching him pull the white T-shirt over his head. This sexy powerful man who comes undone just for me. It's heady, and I'll never get enough of it.

My eyes close when he kisses my neck with the same passion we had the first day.

"Be a good little slut for me, and get on your knees."

I fuck my boss every night in his office.

And I love it.

I love him.

About the Author

Thank you so much for reading my romances. I'm just a stay at home Mom and an avid reader turned Author and I couldn't be happier.

I hope you love my books as much as I do!

More by Willow Winters
www.willowwinterswrites.com/books

Printed in Great Britain
by Amazon